MERLINE LOVELACE

Strangers When We Meet

ROMANTIC
SUSPENSE

ISBN-13: 978-0-373-27730-8

STRANGERS WHEN WE MEET

"Every time I touch you, Larissa Petrovna, I want you more."

"I want, as well. I want to know if this man you spoke of caused the death of my husband and the pain my daughter still suffers. If I must sleep with you to make this happen, I will sleep with you."

"You don't have to sleep with me to make anything happen."

"Oh? And you were not thinking to, as you say, get naked when you opened the door to me?"

"No. Yes. Oh, hell!" He fumbled for the truth. "I desire you, Larissa Petrovna. In ways I don't begin to understand. You fascinate me and challenge me and make me ache to kiss away the lines of strain that mar your face."

Lara stood stiff as a fence post while his thumb traced a light pattern at the corner of her mouth. She couldn't deny the hunger his touch roused.

"I will not lie," she whispered, driven to the truth. "I want your hands on me. I want your body on mine. In mine."

★ ★ ★

Dear Reader,

I first visited F.E. Warren Air Force Base, Wyoming, way back in the dark ages as part of a USAF task force charged with determining whether military women should be assigned to missile duty. I'm proud to say they now pull alert at facilities all across the U.S.

I never forgot the chilling experience of coming face-to-face with a nuclear warhead. Or the wild, windswept beauty of the Wyoming plains. I didn't know then I would use both in a book someday. Now that I have, I hope this story gives you the same feelings of awe and respect I have for the men and women who serve on America's ultimate line of defense.

Merline Lovelace

Books by Merline Lovelace

Romantic Suspense

★*Diamonds Can Be Deadly* #1411
★*Closer Encounters* #1439
★*Stranded with a Spy* #1483
★*Match Play* #1500
★*Undercover Wife* #1531
★*Seduced by the Operative* #1589
★*Risky Engagement* #1613
★*Danger in the Desert* #1640
★*Strangers When We Meet* #1660

Harlequin Nocturne

Mind Games #33
A Christmas Kiss
◊*Time Raiders: The Protector* #75

Desire

★*Devlin and the
   Deep Blue Sea* #1726
★★*The CEO's
   Christmas Proposition* #1905
★★*The Duke's New Year's
   Resolution* #1913
★★*The Executive's Valentine's
   Seduction* #1917

★Code Name: Danger
★★Holidays Abroad
◊Time Raiders

MERLINE LOVELACE

A career Air Force officer, Merline Lovelace served at bases all over the world, including tours in Taiwan, Vietnam and at the Pentagon. When she hung up her uniform for the last time, she decided to combine her love of adventure with a flair for storytelling, basing many of her tales on her experiences in the service.

Since then, she's produced more than eighty action-packed novels, many of which have made *USA TODAY* and Waldenbooks bestseller lists. Over eleven million copies of her works are in print in thirty countries. Be sure to check her website at www.merlinelovelace.com for contests, news and information on future releases.

This book is dedicated to the men and women of the Mighty Ninety, charged with the awesome responsibility of keeping 150 Minuteman III ICBMs on full alert 24-hours a day, 365 days a year. *Impavide!*

Prologue

The annual reception for foreign ambassadors was one of Washington D.C.'s premiere White House events. A string quartet floated exquisite background melodies above conversations held in a host of different languages. White-gloved servers passed among the crowd with silver trays of canapés and sparkling crystal champagne flutes. In addition to diplomats from dozens of nations, the guest list included cabinet members, key congressional leaders and high-powered U.S. agency heads.

Tall, tawny-haired and elegant in his Armani tux, Nick Jensen stood with his wife, Mackenzie. To most of the elite in the room, Jensen was the president's special envoy. The generally meaningless honorific had been bestowed over the years on a succession of wealthy campaign contributors. A mere handful among the glittering assembly knew Nick—code name Lightning—also served as director of OMEGA, an organization so secret that its operatives were activated only by direction of the president himself.

Mackenzie had been active in OMEGA herself until giving birth to twins a few years ago. So had the two people who crossed the room to greet her and Nick. Mac's eyes lit up at the sight of a couple who'd been both mentors and role models for her and her husband.

"Maggie," she said with a rueful smile, "you look too damned gorgeous to be a grandmother."

It was true. Maggie Sinclair Ridgeway showed only a fine trace of lines at the corners of her sparkling brown eyes and a mere touch of silver in her upswept hair. Her gold lamé Versace gown clung to a figure every bit as svelte as that of her daughters. One of those daughters had presented Maggie and her husband, Adam, with ready-made grandkids when she'd adopted two orphans from Hong Kong a few years ago. Soon Gillian would give birth to a third.

The proud granddad slipped an arm around his wife's waist. Adam Ridgeway, code name Thunder, wore his years as easily as Maggie did. His hand-tailored tux showcased a lean, athletic body, and his laser-blue eyes held the same penetrating shrewdness that had made him one of OMEGA's most skilled and lethal operatives before he assumed duties as the agency's director. He now headed the UN's International Monetary Fund while Maggie served as an adjunct professor at Georgetown. The love between them still sizzled in the slow smile Adam gave his wife.

"She looks damned gorgeous, period," he said in response to Mackenzie's observation.

Their shared years at Omega had forged a bond between the two couples that could never be replicated by others who hadn't experienced the chalky taste of fear or exhilarating thrill of pulling off an op against all odds. They reminisced about some of their hairier ops while sipping champagne and sampling the internationally inspired canapés served on silver trays by the White House staff.

A megarich restaurateur in his non-OMEGA life, Nick had just given his stamp of approval to a savory glazed lamb minikebob with Moroccan carrots and tahini puree when he spotted the president with his head bent close to the Russian ambassador's. Although both wore bland smiles, their body language suggested their conversation had veered away from the usual polite chitchat at soirees such as this one.

So Nick wasn't all that surprised when the president's chief of staff made her leisurely way through the crowd some time later and headed in his direction. With a warm smile, the striking brunette acknowledged Maggie, Adam and Mackenzie. Her expression didn't change when she turned to Nick, but the message she conveyed belied her relaxed pose.

"If you don't mind staying a bit after the reception, Lightning, the boss would like to chat with you."

She used his code name in a low murmur that only he and the other three could hear over the chatter and music. Nick nodded, and Adam facilitated the meeting by offering to drive Mac home.

Nick met with the president in his book-lined study in the family residence. John Jefferson Andrews was still lean and fit and boyishly handsome, although the responsibilities of his office had added their share of creases to his face. He'd lost his wife to cancer before he'd run for the presidency. In the view of most of the country, he'd done a damned fine job of raising his teenaged daughter in the fishbowl of the White House. But he would always be grateful to Nick and OMEGA for spoiling a fiendish plot that had played his daughter's mental stability in an attempt to get her worried father to resign during his first year in office.

As a result, his professional relationship with Nick had ripened into a deep and abiding friendship. The ease between them showed in the way Andrews yanked loose his bow tie, let the ends dangle and popped the top button on his pleated shirt before splashing brandy into two crystal snifters.

"I need something to wash down all that sparkling cider," he admitted with a wry smile.

As Nick knew well, the president never indulged in alcohol at social or political functions and rarely drank in private. Andrews flatly refused to risk impairing his judgment when he could be called on to make life-and-death decisions at any moment. That he would allow himself a few sips of the two-thousand-dollar-a-bottle limited-production special cuvée that had been a gift from the French president spoke volumes.

He passed Nick a snifter and held his up in silent salute. The brandy slid down the men's throats like liquid gold. Its mellow fire still lingered on the back of Nick's tongue when Andrews broached the reason for this meeting.

"The Russian ambassador reminded me that their team was gearing up for the first inspection under the new START treaty."

"As if you needed a reminder," Nick commented drily.

All of Washington knew how much political capital the president had expended to push through the new nuclear-arms-reduction pact and how eager his opponents were to see it blow up—metaphorically speaking!—in his face.

"The team will arrive at Francis E. Warren Air Force Base next month."

The president met and held the eyes of his director of OMEGA, each slipping into their respective roles easily.

"I need you to make sure this inspection goes off without a hitch, Lightning. Put your best operatives on it."

"They're all equally skilled," Nick replied without a hint of exaggeration. "But I have one who fits this op like a glove. I'll bring him in tomorrow for prebrief. He'll be primed and in the field when the Russian team arrives."

"Good." Andrews's face was dead serious now. "Last thing I—or the country—needs is for some accident or misunderstanding to kick off a nuclear high noon."

Chapter 1

"How would you like to get back into an air-force flight suit for a few weeks?"

Sloan Hamilton, code name Dodge, smiled wryly as he steered his rented Jeep 4x4 toward the front gate of Francis E. Warren Air Force Base, on the outskirts of Cheyenne, Wyoming. He had the windows open to the cool September air, shimmering with a crystalline clarity. Dodge's thoughts weren't on the purity of his native Wyoming atmosphere, however. Instead, he replayed conversation that had taken place in a windowless control center back in Washington, D.C., just four days ago.

That's all it had taken. One casual suggestion from

Lightning and Dodge had jumped at the chance to get back in the cockpit again. Not that he didn't have plenty of opportunity to fly in his civilian job. The *other* civilian job. The one that didn't involve crashing headfirst through eighth-story windows or being inserted into a damned near impenetrable jungle in pursuit of some sleazoid drug runners. Conducting aerial surveys in his steady, sturdy Cessna wasn't anywhere near as much fun as piloting an air-force UH-1N, though. The helo was Vietnam-era vintage, but after several generations of modifications it was still the best and most reliable chopper in the air.

As it turned out, Dodge should have asked for a little more detail before accepting this assignment. Instead of driving a Huey, he was about to undertake what looked to be one of his tamest missions for OMEGA—riding herd on a three-person Russian team that would arrive in Cheyenne tomorrow to inspect U.S. Minuteman III missiles in accordance with the new START treaty.

True, the president had just signed the treaty after more than a decade of fierce negotiations between Russia and the U.S. Also true, recent tensions between the U.S. and Russia had made this first inspection under the new protocols a matter of intense interest at the highest national security levels. Still, Dodge would have much preferred a task that involved flying his old bird to babysitting a Russian major and her two teammates.

Even a Russian major who looked like this one.

He glanced at the file on the passenger seat. Clipped to its outside was a brief bio that included a head-and-shoulders shot of Larissa Katerina Petrovna. The fact that the photo was in black and white and a little grainy in no way detracted from the major's ice-maiden beauty. Her hair looked as pale as fine champagne. Her wide-spaced eyes stared back at Dodge from above a straight, aristocratic nose. Her mouth was full and ripe and downright sensual.

He knew from the detailed briefing he'd received at OMEGA headquarters, before departing for Cheyenne, that those eyes were electric-blue. He also knew the puckered skin on the left side of Petrovna's neck and jaw were the result of horrific burns she'd suffered in the apartment fire that had killed her husband and almost claimed her baby girl.

Dodge felt a flicker of sympathy, quickly doused. A female didn't make it to the rank of major in any air force, Russia's included, by being soft or welcoming expressions of sympathy. And judging by the jobs Larissa Petrovna held on her way up the ranks, the woman was tough as nails. More to the point, she was here to do a specific task.

So was Dodge, although he had to admit, being

back in Wyoming was almost as much of a plus as being back in uniform. His gaze shifted to the snow-and-pine-covered mountains on the horizon. They looked close enough to reach out and touch, but he knew how deceptive the expanse of rolling plain between here and those jagged peaks could be. He should. He'd ridden fence lines on these wind- and snow-swept plains often enough.

He'd grown up just a little over an hour north of here. He and his cousin Sam. Closer than brothers, they'd tickled trout in mountain streams and brought cattle down from the high country each fall. They'd also eaten their share of dirt after being bucked off angry bulls and mean-tempered broncs while competing in rodeos in and around Cheyenne. Sam was the one who'd hung Dodge's nickname on him, commenting laconically that his cuz was a whole lot better at dodging bulls' horns than staying on their backs.

Grimacing over the memory of how close one particular set of horns had come to gelding him, Dodge wheeled through Francis E. Warren's gate one. Just inside the gate stood three gleaming white missiles, mute testimony to the base's current mission.

A legacy of President Lincoln's plan to establish a transcontinental railroad, the original outpost had been established in the 1870s to protect Union-Pacific workers from hostile Indians. Gradually, it had grown into the largest cavalry post in the nation. Troopers assigned to the fort had endured the bone-biting winter winds that howled across the plains, participated in the Great Sioux Indian Wars and over the years watched their role transform from cavalry to field artillery to airplanes to sleek, intercontinental ballistic missiles.

Now, the 90th Missile Wing headquartered at Warren controlled a lethal arsenal of Minuteman III missiles spread across twelve thousand square miles of Wyoming, Colorado and Nebraska. The Mighty Ninety, as it was known in air-force parlance, took its nuclear mission very, very seriously. There was zero tolerance for mistakes in judgment when you controlled the launch codes for ICBMs.

Making a left turn onto Old Glory Road, Dodge followed the traffic flow down a sloping hill to the marshy lowlands of Crow Creek, then back up to the newer part of the base. A few more turns took him to the tan-colored, corrugated-tin building that housed the 37th Helicopter Flight. He found a parking space and clamped a hand on his flight cap to anchor it during the short walk to the door.

Luckily, he'd retained his status in the reserves. When the Russians checked him out, as he knew they would, his cover was that he'd been recalled to active duty because of critical manpower shortages due to the 37th's support of operations in Iraq and Afghanistan. To give substance to that cover, Dodge had arrived at the base two days ago and gone through refresher training on the Huey. Although his escort duties didn't require him to fly, even the most cursory check of flight records would show that Major Sloan "Dodge" Hamilton was current in all phases of the UH-1N.

Dumping his gear in the large, open room that served as the pilots' office, he snatched a cup of coffee and headed down the hall to check the operations center status board. With luck, he might snag another few hours in the cockpit before he went into babysitting mode.

"Hey, Major." The duty officer manning the ops desk gave him a message instead of another flight. "The CO wants to see you."

Nodding, Dodge retraced his steps through the corridors to the flight commander's office. He'd known Lt. Colonel Sean McGee for years, had flown with him back when they were both gung ho lieutenants doing combat rescue. Dodge greeted his friend back with the irreverent graveyard humor that had earned McGee his nickname.

"Morning, Digger. You want to see me?"

"Not me. Colonel Yarboro."

Dodge's brows lifted. "The Mighty Ninety commander? Why?"

"His exec didn't offer any specifics. Just said Yarboro wants you to report to his office." Propping a boot on an open desk drawer, McGee tilted back in his chair. "Might have something to do with my suggestion, though."

"The one that involves my permanent transition back from civilian status?" Dodge asked with a smile.

"That's the one."

"Wish I could oblige."

McGee knew Dodge now ran his own aerial-survey company. He didn't, however, know about his work for OMEGA. The agency was so secret that few people outside of a trusted handful were even aware of its existence.

"Think about it," McGee urged. "You haven't lost your touch. My guys tell me you aced both checkrides."

"Yeah, well," Dodge drawled in the Wyoming twang he'd never quite shed. "Flyin' a Huey's like makin' love to a beautiful woman. Once you get her out of the chocks, everything else comes naturally."

McGee grinned. "You've sure as hell gotten more than your share out of the chocks. And escaped their clutches afterward. You and I both know your handle doesn't come just from dodging bulls."

Dodge kept his smile in place and let the comment slide. He'd loved once, or thought he had. The memory could still slice into him when he let it.

"I'd better go see what the colonel wants."

He reported in to the commander of the 90th Missile Wing fifteen moments later. Seated behind a desk roughly the size of Kansas, Colonel Yarboro returned his salute and waved him to a seat.

"You ready for the Russian team?"

"Yes, sir."

The colonel's eyes raked him from head to toe. Good thing Dodge had had his shaggy brown hair trimmed and boots buffed. OMEGA undercover operatives tended more toward comfort than spit and polish when in the field. Rejoining the air force, even temporarily, had called for some spiffing up.

Yarboro was only one of three people who'd been read in on the real reason for Dodge's sudden appearance at F. E. Warren. Everyone else had been fed the cover story. The colonel wasn't happy about having an outsider foisted on him, though. Even one with Major Sloan Hamilton's military and civilian credentials.

"Before you make contact with Major Petrovna," he

said brusquely, "I want to make sure you understand who you're up against."

Yarboro lifted a typed sheet and skimmed down the page. A career missileer who'd worked his way up from launch officer to commander of the world's most sophisticated ICBM force, he targeted the salient items with pinpoint accuracy.

"Born, Bryansk. Age 33. Widowed. One child. Attended the Gagarin Air Force Academy. Holds advanced degrees in both math and astrophysics."

That would strike a cord with the colonel, Dodge guessed. Yarboro had earned a doctorate from MIT in astrophysics himself.

"She pulled a tour as a relatively junior officer at strike-force headquarters in Moscow, then commanded a SS-18 squadron."

Those accomplishments didn't exactly endear her to either Dodge or the colonel. The missile officers assigned to the 90th spent twenty-four hours at a stretch some eighty feet below the ground, locked behind eight-ton blast doors while they played a deadly game of chicken with their Russian counterparts. The cold war might have ended for the rest of the world. It hadn't cooled more than a few degrees for the men and women charged with the nerve-twisting task of nuclear deterrence.

"Petrovna spent the past four years at various

staff jobs," Yarboro continued, "including two with the research-and-development directorate. Word is that Colonel Zacharov, head of Russian military intelligence, handpicked her to head this special team because of her expertise."

Dodge kept silent. He knew Petrovna's background as well as the colonel did. There was a reason Yarboro was reiterating her credentials. Probably had to do with the fact that Washington had sent Dodge in to bird-dog her instead of using one of the locals.

"When you meet Petrovna and her team at the airport this afternoon, you'll bring her by here for a courtesy call," Yarboro instructed. "Tom Jordan, our treaty compliance officer, will conduct the orientation briefing at oh-eight-hundred tomorrow morning. He's lined up additional escorts to take care of the other two team members."

"Yes, sir."

Yarboro leaned forward, his eyes intent. "This is the first inspection under the new START treaty. I don't need to tell you how important it is."

The new START.

The acronym didn't quite fit, Dodge thought cynically, since the Strategic Arms Reduction Treaty just signed by the presidents of the U.S. and the Russian Federation was the third treaty by that name. Each iteration had led to a reduction of nuclear warheads and strategic delivery systems, but the two superpowers still fielded some fifteen hundred nuclear warheads each.

"The top dogs on both sides will be watching," Yarboro warned. "We don't want any screwups."

Dodge didn't remind him that was why the president had tapped OMEGA to send someone in.

"No, sir."

"Just get the Russians where they need to go, when they need to go. And make sure they observe the inspection protocol." Yarboro thumped a thick binder sitting on the side of his desk. "I assume you've read it."

Yeah, he'd read it. Its title was as mind-numbing as its dozens of chapters.

Protocol to the Treaty Between the United States of America and the Russian Federation on Measures for the Further Reduction and Limitation of Strategic Offensive Arms

The document covered everything from the on-site verification of active nuclear assets to the disposal of warheads taken out of service. Then there was the section labeled Escort Officer Duties, with separate tabs for housing, transportation, meals, clothing, handling of equipment and contacts with the media. The damned volume had taken most of four hours to get through.

"According to the protocol, I'm supposed to do everything but wipe the major's nose," Dodge commented.

"You do that, too, if necessary."

Looked to be a fun couple of weeks, he mused, as the colonel continued.

"I want you to keep two key points in mind, Hamilton. One, Major Petrovna communicates her team's needs through you and *only* through you. Two, the treaty accords these people what amounts to diplomatic status. Their quarters, work area and papers are sacrosanct. And while they're expected to abide by the host-country laws, they enjoy a high degree of immunity."

"Right."

The two men's eyes locked. They both knew the Russians were charged with the collateral mission of gathering intelligence on U.S. systems.

"Previous team members have been observed dropping pencils or pens at missile sites," Yarboro commented. "When they bend down to retrieve the fallen article, they scoop up a soil sample for later analysis. And many pretend they can't speak English, in hopes of overhearing chance conversations, although their biographies clearly indicate a facility with the language."

"I know the major is fluent in English," Dodge commented. "The others with her not so much."

"Captain Tyschenko can get by," Yaroboro confirmed. "Aleksei Bugarin speaks German and French, as well as some English. But be particularly careful what you say to him. He's FSB."

FSB—Federal Security Service—Russia's modern-day successor to the KGB. If half of what Dodge had read about KGB tactics held even a grain of truth, they'd been one bad bunch of boys and girls. FSB was proving itself worse.

"Bugarin's job is to keep a close eye on the other members of the team and report immediately any suspicious activity," Yarboro stated succinctly. "Your job is to do the same."

To Dodge's surprise, the colonel unbent enough to give a flinty smile.

"I'm as familiar with your background, Hamilton, as I am with Major Petrovna's. I don't think you'll have any trouble handling the team."

Dodge didn't think so, either. Right up until the jet carrying the team taxied up to the air-national-guard side of the Cheynne airport late that afternoon.

He was waiting inside the terminal with the two other members of the escort team. Lieutenant Benjamin Tate was an earnest young officer, proud of both his shiny missileer badge and his African-American heritage. Senior Master Sergeant Lewis sported a shock of red hair, five rows of ribbons on his uniform jacket and a sleeve full of stripes. Given his years of experience, he'd been assigned to escort Aleksei Bugarin, the FSB officer. Dodge kept an eye on the passengers exiting the craft and ran through a final list of dos and don'ts.

"Remember, we're not supposed to get too friendly with these guys. Don't let them take any pictures without prior approval. Don't exchange gifts, except small trinkets like coffee mugs or unit patches, and be sure to run any trinket the Russians offer you by the Office of Special Investigations to have it checked for bugs. And don't make any physical contact, except to prevent serious injury."

"Roger that," Sergeant Lewis acknowledged.

"There they are," the lieutenant murmured.

Dodge had no difficulty identifying Major Petrovna when she appeared. The treaty required inspection personnel to wear civilian clothes while visiting a host country, but even in her badly cut navy suit, she was striking. She wore her silver-blond hair pulled back in a high twist that emphasized her sculpted cheekbones. A decidedly aristocratic nose gave her an elegant air, at odds with that lush, sensual mouth.

When she got closer, Dodge saw that her eyes were blue, as her bio had indicated. A deep purplish-blue, almost the same color as the monkshood that blanketed the high valleys in spring—also known as wolfsbane, women's bane, the Devil's helmet and the blue rocket, Dodge reminded himself wryly. Highly toxic if the roots were ingested. Something he'd best remember.

Those intense blue eyes flicked over him, taking in his height, stance and uniform in a quick, assessing glance before moving to the two men with him. As she approached, Dodge spotted the puckered skin on the left side of her neck and lower jaw. Not even that spiderweb tracery of scars could detract from the overall package.

The look she gave him as he extended his hand was another story. It went past cool and hovered somewhere around icy.

"Welcome to Cheyenne, Major Petrovna. I'm Dodge Hamilton."

She gave his hand a brisk shake, after which they took turns introducing the others. Then she got right to the point in heavily accented English.

"My team requires transportation to their quarters. You will arrange it, then escort me to call upon Colonel Yarboro so I may present my credentials."

Although the clipped instructions coincided exactly with Dodge's intentions, that imperious "will" had him lifting a brow. The lady was obviously used to being in charge.

"Lieutenant Tate and Sergeant Lewis will help your folks with the baggage and drive them to their quarters," he replied. "If you'll come with me, I'll take you directly to the wing headquarters."

Leading the way, he escorted his charge out of the terminal to the blue air-force sedan parked at the curb and opened the passenger-side door. Petrovna slid into her seat without so much as a nod or word of thanks.

If the grueling flight from Moscow and nine-hour time differential had sapped the major's energy, she didn't allow it to show. Sitting ramrod straight in the passenger seat, she answered Dodge's polite question about her flight in curt monosyllables, and displayed no trace of weariness during the fifteen-minute drive from the airport.

Her blue eyes absorbed Cheyenne's rolling landscape, then locked on the tall, white missiles standing sentry at the base's front gate. When the gate guard had waved them through and the white-trimmed brick buildings of the old fort appeared, Dodge made another attempt to break the ice.

"The base started life as a cavalry post. It's part of our wild-and-woolly Western heritage."

"I know this," Petrovna replied repressively. "I haf been…" She stopped, corrected herself. "I have been here before, on an inspection team under the old treaty."

So much for that conversational gambit. Flicking the directional signal, Dodge turned into the parking lot beside the two-story brick building that housed the headquarters of the 90th Space Wing. Once parked, he reached behind him for a fat envelope.

"This contains your identification badge, a base directory and a paper copy of the slides that will be presented at the in-brief tomorrow."

He passed over the package. The major accepted it without comment.

"You should wear the badge whenever you're on base."

With a look that said she was perfectly aware of the protocol, Petrovna clipped the plastic identifier to the lapel of her navy suit jacket and didn't wait for Dodge to come around and open her door.

Her low-heeled black pumps beat a precise tattoo on the sidewalk as she led the way to the head-quarters' front entrance. Sturdy outer wooden doors opened into a glassed-in foyer, designed to break the force of Wyoming's constant winds. Once inside the foyer, security forces checked their badges and handheld articles before waving them through.

Some kind of high-powered meeting had just broken up, Dodge saw. A small crowd of civilians in expensive-looking suits and power ties were just filing past the security checkpoint. The badges dangling from their suit pockets identified them as contractors. Dodge picked up bits and pieces of conversation as the group passed.

"The Pentagon's still working the RFP."

"…won't release the initial specs until January."

"We're talking five, maybe six years for development, integration and testing."

The last speaker had already passed, but his voice snagged Dodge's attention. It was low and rough. Almost rasping. As if someone had punched the man in the throat and he was still getting his wind back.

"I don't see it happening," Gritty Voice was saying, "before…"

"Ummph!"

With a startled grunt, Dodge collided with the woman who'd stopped in her tracks just ahead of him. The force of the collision propelled Petrovna into a near free fall. He lunged forward and caught her just in time.

Whoa! There was a real woman under those layers of permafrost. Dodge didn't exactly cop a feel. He had a little more class than that. Besides, there was the treaty's explicit prohibition against touching. But he certainly registered a set of long, sinuous curves under her shapeless navy suit.

"Sorry 'bout that." Reluctantly, he set her on her feet. "Colonel Yarboro's office is straight ahead."

Instead of moving on, the Russian pivoted slowly.

"This way, Major Petrovna."

She paid no attention. She stood rooted in place, staring at the backs of the departing men. Every trace of color had drained from her face. Her blue eyes were glassy with shock.

Chapter 2

"Major?"

Petrovna didn't respond. She'd gone so pale that the puckered skin on her neck and lower jaw stood out like the shadowed craters of the moon.

"Major Petrovna? Are you okay?"

Dazed blue eyes swung toward Dodge. *"Shto?"*

"Are you all right?"

The blonde didn't answer. She stared blankly at him for several seconds, then pushed past. Backtracking through security, she shoved open the door to the building's exterior and searched the crowd now climbing into various vehicles. Whatever she saw didn't appear to satisfy her. Spinning around, she fired off a torrent of Russian.

"Sorry," Dodge said. "I don't understand."

With an obvious effort, she fought to recall her English. "Did you see him?"

"See who?"

"The one who speaks... How do you say? Like a... Like a..."

"You mean the guy who growled like a dog?"

"Yes! The one who growls like the dog. Did you see him?"

"I heard him, but I didn't see him."

"Do you know who he is, this one?"

Dodge didn't have a clue, but he sure as hell intended to find out.

"From their badges," he said slowly, "I'd guess he was part of a group of civilian contractors."

He waited for her to explain. When she didn't, he pressed her. "What's with the growler? Have you crossed swords with him before or something?"

"What do you say?"

"Obviously, you recognized that guy's voice. How do you know him?"

"I..."

Petrovna lifted a hand. The fingers she pressed against her scars were trembling, Dodge noted with a sudden kink in his gut.

"I once…"

"You once what?"

The question seemed to recall her from wherever her racing thoughts had taken her. Abruptly, she dropped her hand. Beneath the rumpled suit jacket, her shoulders stiffened.

"I think perhaps I hear a voice like this one before. I make the mistake." Turning, she marched down the hall. "Come, we will be late for my appointment."

"Hold on!"

Dodge caught up with her in three quick steps. When she refused to slow, he said to hell with the rules and snagged her arm.

"You looked as if you were about to pass out on me a moment ago. Why did hearing that growl almost buckle your knees?"

"I make the mistake."

She glanced down pointedly at his hand. When she lifted her gaze again, she could have chipped granite with her flinty stare.

"We waste time. Come."

Stiff-spined, she swept down the hall. Dodge trailed her, swallowing a few decidedly uncomplimentary remarks about Russians in general, and tight-assed Russian majors in particular.

They were ushered into the 90th Missile Wing commander's office a few minutes later. Although the major maintained her stiff, professional manner, she unbent a little during the courtesy call. Once, she even smiled. Just a polite curve of her lips, but even so, the transformation was startling.

Well, damn! Good thing she didn't do that more often, Dodge thought. Her snow-princess looks were enough to make a man start thinking of ways to initiate a spring melt. When she thawed even a few degrees, his thoughts took a sharp jump into long, hot summer nights.

The brief thaw probably had a lot to do with the fact that she and the colonel spoke the same missile-ese. Within minutes, the two astrophysicists had left Dodge behind in the technical dust.

When they were joined by the vice-commander, Dodge used the cover of polite conversation to slip into the outer office and pop a question at the colonel's administrative assistant.

"Can I ask a favor, ma'am?"

"Sure."

"When Major Petrovna and I entered the headquarters building a little while ago, we passed a passel of civilian contractors. Would you check and see if there was a meeting or briefing in the conference room they might have been attending? If so, I need the name and telephone number of the officer who set it up."

"No problem."

She punched a button on her intercom. Within moments, she'd obtained the requested information from the conference-room scheduler.

"It was a briefing on the proposed new exo-atmospheric defense system," she informed Dodge. "Lieutenant Colonel Haskell from the plans directorate conducted it."

She scribbled his name, office symbol and phone number on a pink memo slip.

"Thanks."

Stuffing the slip into a zippered pocket of his uniform, Dodge waited for Petrovna to make her farewells. Once they were back in the sedan and headed for the quarters set aside for the visiting team, he tried again.

"About the voice you heard in the hallway. You sure you don't want to tell me why it spooked you?"

Petrovna's jaw clenched, stretching her scarred skin tight over the bone. "I make the mistake. We will speak no more of it."

Wrong. They would speak about it a whole lot more, once Dodge got a tag on Dog Voice.

"You will take me to my quarters so I may rest from the flight," she announced coldly. "Tomorrow, you will report at oh-six-hundred. We must breakfast before the in-brief."

"Yes, ma'am," he drawled, with just enough of an edge to cause her to cut him a quick look.

"You must escuse me if I sound…" She waved a hand, searching for the right word. "If I sound…"

"Uptight?" Dodge supplied helpfully. "Like maybe you sat on the pointy end of a missile?"

Her jaw dropped. She stared at him for several seconds before a gleam of what looked suspiciously like laughter lit her eyes. She controlled the impulse before it could make it to her lips.

"You will excuse me," she said again, repressively. "It has been a long day."

Dodge figured that was as close as he was going to get to an apology. Nodding, he cut through the traffic headed off base and circled the parade ground. Stately homes left over from the cavalry days lined two sides of the meticulously mowed field. On the south end were the long, low buildings that once had housed unmarried cavalry officers. They now served as Visiting Officers' Quarters.

The buildings' exterior retained the look of the 1880s. The redbrick walls, tin roof and long, white-painted porches were all original. Successive renovations, however, had brought the interiors up to modern comfort standards. Each suite contained a living room and bedroom, with a bath and small kitchenette tucked into the hallway between the two.

The sofa and chairs were upholstered in earth-toned fabrics, and the accessories scattered around the rooms reflected Warren's frontier heritage. Lamps made of welded horseshoes sat on the end tables. A shadow box displaying crossed cavalry swords hung above the campaign-style desk. Framed prints and wide windows brought Wyoming's spectacular mountains and rolling plains into the room.

In keeping with his cover of a reservist recalled to active duty to assist during severe pilot shortages, Dodge was quartered in the VOQ across the parking lot. He would have preferred to bunk down with his cousin Sam on the Double H, but the ranch was more than an hour's drive north of Cheyenne. This arrangement let him keep a closer eye on his charge.

He'd checked the major's suite earlier to make sure the cupboards were stocked and the protocol office had delivered the prerequisite gift basket. It sat on the coffee table as Petrovna skimmed a quick glance around the living room and dropped her briefcase on the desk. After ascertaining that her suitcase had already arrived, she confirmed the room numbers assigned to her teammates before dismissing her escort.

"I will see you tomorrow."

Dodge ignored the brush-off. The woman intrigued

him in more ways than one. With her odd reaction at wing headquarters front and center in his mind, he tendered a casual invitation.

"The pantry's stocked with soup and such, but I could pick up you and your folks after you've rested and take you to dinner."

"We ate the sandwich on the airplane."

"You're sure?"

"Da." The blonde held out an impatient hand for the key. "You may leave now. And…" As if recalled to her manners, she gave him a quick nod. "I thank you."

"You're welcome."

Her brief spate of cordiality ended, she dismissed him once again. "I will see you tomorrow."

Damn straight she would, Dodge thought as he tipped two fingers to his forehead in a casual salute.

It took every bit of Lara's iron discipline to keep her face expressionless and her voice steady until the door closed behind the American officer.

As soon as it shut, her discipline imploded and the tremors she'd fought with every ounce of her being took over. Her arms and legs began to shake. Her breath shortened to strangled gasps that cut through the silence of the suite like a Cossack saber.

That voice! That rasping growl! It couldn't be the same one she'd heard that horrific night. It couldn't.

Blindly, she groped her way to the nearest chair and collapsed. Her breath razored from her lungs through a throat clogged tight. As if it were yesterday, she could feel the heat scorching her face, her hands. Feel the paralyzing panic as the wall of fire roared toward her. She'd screamed for Yuri, for Katya. Dragging off her heavy military overcoat, she'd wrapped it around her head and was about to plunge through the wall when her husband burst through the flames with their baby daughter in his arms.

Lara didn't cry. Not anymore. She hadn't since the night her husband died in her arms. But she couldn't hold back an agonized groan as she rocked in the chair and tried to force the searing memories back into the black corner of her soul where they would always live.

Larissa Petrovna was front and center in Dodge's mind when he pushed through the door at the end of the long hall and stepped into an early dusk. The ever-present Wyoming wind nipped at his face and hands as he walked past the blue sedan he'd been assigned for the duration of the Russians' visit. He would have preferred to chauffeur the major around in his rented 4x4, but protocol dictated a vehicle with USAF markings and license plates for their official duties.

His quarters were just across the parking lot. The rooms were similar in design and layout to Petrovna's, and a hell of a lot more comfortable than some of the rat holes he'd occupied during other ops. As he keyed the lock, he kept returning to that business outside the wing commander's office. What the heck was that all about?

Tossing his hat and keys on the table, he checked his watch. Just a little past six. He fished out the piece of paper with the number jotted down by the wing commander's administrative assistant. Colonel Haskell had probably left for the day, but Dodge decided to give him a call anyway.

Haskell picked up on the third ring. He was, he informed Dodge, just on his way out the door.

"Then I'll make this quick. I understand you gave a briefing at wing headquarters this afternoon."

"That's right. The subject of the briefing wasn't classified, but I'll tell you right up front I can't discuss any of the specific issues we addressed over an open phone line."

"I'm more interested in the attendees than the issues. One attendee in particular. A civilian con-tractor."

"There were upward of thirty contractors in the room."

"This one spoke in a low, sort of rasping voice, as if he had something stuck in the back of his throat."

"I know who you mean. His name's Hank Barlow. He's the CEO of E-Systems." He paused a moment. "What's your interest in him?"

Dodge fully intended to report Major Petrovna's reaction to this guy Barlow. It had been too odd to let pass. He'd confine his report to those with a need to know, though.

"I heard his voice as he was going out of the headquarters and I was coming in," he said easily. "Thought I knew him from somewhere and was curious as to his identity."

"Now you know. Want me to track down his number for you?"

"That's okay. I can get it. Thanks."

He hung up and made two additional calls. The first was to the Office of Special Investigations. The OSI conducted counterintelligence ops within the air force, in addition to investigating everything from terrorism to desertion, drug trafficking and/or murder.

The local OSI duty officer patched him through immediately to the F. E. Warren detachment commander, Lt. Colonel Paul Handerhand. Handerhand listened without comment when Dodge described Major Petrovna's odd behavior, and promised to have his people check out Hank Barlow.

"I'll do the same," Dodge advised.

That was met with a short silence. Handerhand had been read-in on some of Dodge's background and knew he'd been brought in from an outside agency. That was all he knew.

"Let me know what you find out," Handerhand said briskly.

"Same goes."

Dodge disconnected and pressed the star key on his cell phone. The instrument looked ordinary enough, but Mackenzie Blair Jensen, the agency's guru of all things electronic, had crammed in enough circuitry to bounce signals off a supernova. The device also performed an instant thumbprint, iris scan and voice analysis to identify the user's biometrics and detect if he or she was under duress before connecting to OMEGA's control center.

The high-tech control center was located on the third floor of a town house in the heart of Washington D.C.'s embassy district. All a casual passerby would see if they strolled past the town house was a discreet bronze plaque identifying the building as home to the offices of the President's Special Envoy. The title was one of those empty honorifics dreamed up to give a wealthy campaign contributor a chance to rub elbows with Washington's movers and shakers. A mere handful of insiders knew that the President's Special Envoy also served as director of OMEGA. As such, he fielded highly trained and specialized agents, only at the direction of the president and only when it wasn't expedient to use other, more established agencies.

Which said a lot about Washington's determination to make sure this START III inspection went off without a glitch. With the international situation so precarious and wild-eyed insurgents blowing themselves up all around the world, the last thing either the U.S. or Russia needed was an incident that could lead to a nuclear showdown.

Feeling the weight of all those nukes on his shoulders, Dodge held the cell phone up so the scanner could beam his iris print. Seconds later, his controller's face painted across the screen.

"Hey, Dodger."

"Hey yourself, Blade."

Clint Black, code name Blade, had been with OMEGA almost as long as Dodge himself. They'd worked several ops together and would trust each other with their lives. That trust didn't extend to women, though. Blade was still plotting payback for the fun-loving UPI reporter Dodge had whisked out from under his nose last year.

Although…Dodge and everyone else at OMEGA had been watching with some interest the fireworks that sparked between Blade and one of the newer agents. The betting was Blade's sharp edge was about to get blunted, big-time.

"How's it going out there in cowboy country?"

"It's going," Dodge replied.

After a succinct status report that included his initial impressions of the three Russians, he broached the reason for his call.

"I need you to check out a dude by the name of Hank Barlow. He's the CEO of E-Systems."

"Hank Barlow. E-Systems. Got it. Anything in particular you want me to look for?"

"See if he has any connection to our visiting Russians."

"Roger that. I'll get back to you."

Blade hung up and keyed the name into OMEGA's computers. While the supercomputer did its thing, he skimmed a glance around the busy control center.

It was geared to operate 24/7. Active and passive electronic countermeasures prevented interception of its encrypted emanations. Communications techs kept the array of computers and wall-size digital displays humming. Even the field-dress unit, which could turn a grungy agent just back from three weeks in the jungle into a tuxedoed James Bond in the blink of an eye, had at least one team member working some esoteric disguise or another.

Blade dragged his chair closer to the operations control panel to key in the name of the individual and company Dodge had just requested data on. Blade intended to run both through a wire-tight screen. He'd done enough covert ops for OMEGA to know success or failure on any mission hung by a thread. A late contact, a small detail buried under others, a blurred photo—any or all of them could spell disaster. He'd just started skimming the info that came when his nemesis strolled in.

"Oh, Christ."

Victoria Talbot, code name Rebel, caught the low mutter and pasted on a saccharine smile.

"Good to see you, too."

Blade blew out a slow breath and swung around to face the honey-haired operative. She was dressed in her usual leather: bomber jacket, thigh-hugging pants, boots, all the same thin, supple black. All she needed to complete the image of an oversexed biker babe were a few tattoos.

It wasn't that Blade disliked the woman. Hell, the truth was, she turned him on. But they'd had this love/hate thing going ever since they'd clashed during Rebel's first week at OMEGA. It had been a simple misunderstanding, for Christ's sake. She didn't need to knock Blade flat on his ass. Wouldn't have, if he'd had the least inkling she would even try.

They were both professionals. They'd smoothed things over. On the surface, at least. But they both knew whatever the hell was going on beneath that surface would blow up in their faces one of these days.

"You need something?" he asked, with a credible attempt at civility.

"No. Just wanted to check on Dodge." She cranked her too-sweet smile up another notch. "I thought I could help, since he and I are both former air force."

And Blade wasn't. Obviously she thought his stint as a lowly army special-forces grunt didn't count for squat when dealing with one of her fellow hotshot pilots.

"Thanks anyway, but I've got it under control."

"You sure?" Her glance flicked from him to the screen. What she saw there made her lift a brow. "Hank Barlow? Is that the E-Systems guy?"

She crowded closer to peer at the screen. *Too close, dammit.* Blade got a whiff of her scent as she leaned over his shoulder. How the hell could leather smell so sexy?

"E-Systems," she murmured. "Yep, that's him."

Much as it galled him, Blade had to ask. "You know him?"

Rebel hitched a hip on the console, forcing him to scoot his chair back to give her room.

"I hauled Barlow across the pond a couple times when I was still flying VIP transport," she commented. "He was heading some high-powered trade delegation. Had ambassador status, or something close to it. Why are you checking him out?"

"Dodge says he's at F. E. Warren."

"So?"

He stifled the urge to tell her this was his op and she could take herself and those come-get-me leathers elsewhere. Talbot might rub him exactly the wrong way, but she was as good at this business as any operative he'd ever worked with.

"One of the members of the Russian inspection team froze up after a chance encounter with Barlow. Dodge wanted me to see if the man has a connection to Moscow."

"I can answer that," she said with only a trace of smugness. "The trade delegation I just mentioned? They were negotiating with the Russians."

Chapter 3

Dodge was still chewing over the information Blade had relayed when he crossed the parking lot between the VOQs at oh-dark-thirty the next morning. The insulated bomber-style jacket he wore over his flight suit provided more than adequate protection from the predawn chill, but not from the doubts swirling around inside his head.

Blade had confirmed Larissa Petrovna's presence in Moscow during at least three of Barlow's visits to that city. What was their connection? And why had she denied there *was* one? OMEGA was digging deeper into Barlow's background. In the meantime,

Dodge would do his damndest to find out what was going on behind the major's ice-maiden facade.

Lieutenant Tate and Senior Master Sergeant Lewis were waiting at the entrance to the VOQ. They peeled off to collect their charges, and Dodge rapped on Petrovna's door. When she answered, he almost did a double take. The woman looked like a ghost in the dim light spilling into the hallway. Purple circles shadowed her eyes. Tired lines were etched into her face. She wore a black turtleneck sweater under the jacket of her navy suit instead of yesterday's white blouse. The dark shades contrasted cruelly with her pallor.

Jet lag must have smacked the major right between the eyes. Or was her obviously restless night connected to her knee-jerk reaction yesterday? Dodge's gut told him it was the latter, but he kept his expression polite and his voice casual as he offered a choice of breakfast establishments.

"There's a Burger King on base as well as the chow hall. Or we could drive into town if you prefer."

"The dining facility is best. I will get my briefcase, then we go."

She left the door standing open while she disappeared into the bedroom. Dodge was careful not to step inside uninvited. The treaty protocol had emphasized that inspectors' living quarters were to be accorded the inviolability given to the private residences of diplomatic agents.

Dodge's duties as an escort required him to make sure the major's basic needs were taken care of, however. He scanned the living area with a quick glance. Interesting that Petrovna hadn't yet left her mark on the room. No clothes or books lay scattered over the furniture. No dirty dishes sat in the sink or on the kitchen counter.

The only personal item of any kind was the eight-by-ten framed photo on the desk. The photographer had captured a pigtailed girl of five or six. She was holding a kitten up to the camera. Her gap-toothed grin was so mischievous that it drew an answering smile from Dodge.

"Pretty little girl," he commented when the major walked back into the living room.

Her glance went to the photo. "So do I think."

"Is she your daughter?"

He wasn't prepared for the effect the simple question produced. Before his eyes, Larissa Petrovna's face softened and a hint of a smile curved her mouth.

"Da. That is my Katya."

Well, damn! The woman was a stunner even when encased in ice. Without it, she took on a transcendent beauty. Hoping to prolong the transformation, Dodge ventured another observation.

"She looks like she's a handful. A youngster with a lively spirit," he interpreted, at her questioning look.

"A most lively spirit." Her almost-smile turned rueful. "She does not understand the meaning of *nyet,* that one."

For a few dangerous moments, Dodge stopped thinking of Larissa Petrovna as a Russian and the target he'd been sent to keep in his sights. She looked all too human as she gazed at the photo of her daughter. Human, and surprisingly fragile.

Everyone had their weak point, some family secret or prized possession or passion that made them vulnerable. Dodge's years in the field had taught him a number of innovative—and occasionally brutal—ways to discover and exploit those weaknesses. Yet as he studied Petrovna's face, he found himself hoping he wouldn't have to exploit this particular weakness.

That thought stayed with him as he escorted her through the predawn darkness to the sedan. The temperature inside the vehicle was as cold as it was outside. From the corner of his eye, he caught the series of shivers that wracked his passenger.

"Do you want to go back to your room for a coat?"

"No."

"You sure? It's supposed to warm up this afternoon, but the weather around here's pretty unpredictable."

"I am sure. You will drive, please."

Dodge put the sedan in gear and waited for the engine to warm before he flipped on the heater. The hot air that gushed out would soon have him sweating under his flight suit and jacket, but he figured a little perspiration was better than nursing Larissa Petrovna through a bout of pneumonia.

They waited for the other team members and escorts to claim their vehicles, then drove to the dining facility. Major Petrovna took a tray from the stack at the end of the self-serve counter and proceeded to fill a coffee mug and a plate with modest helpings of sliced peaches, scrambled eggs and bacon. Her teammates, however, appeared stunned by the array of choices offered. They broke into excited Russian and heaped plates and bowls to overflowing. Dodge took last place in line and signed the meal chit for the team.

Petrovna ate sparingly and watched with barely disguised distaste as the heavyset Aleksei Bugarin went back for seconds, then thirds. The scarred skin on the side of her chin was drawn tight when she glanced pointedly at her watch.

"It grows late," she told the FSB officer coolly. "We must leave."

Bugarin swiped the last of the gravy from his plate with two slices of bread, crammed them into his mouth and nodded.

The in-brief at the 90th Missile Wing headquarters lasted for more than two hours. The wing battle staff filled the high-backed blue chairs around the oval conference table, with three seats reserved at the table for the Russian team. Dodge sat beside his charge, Lieutenant Tate and SMSgt. Lewis behind theirs.

Tom Jordan, the wing's treaty compliance officer, took the podium to the left of the oval conference table. Major Petrovna took the podium to the right. As the sides came up on screen, Jordan briefed it and the major translated it into Russian for her teammates. They began with a detailed recap of the provisions of the new START treaty and progressed to an even more detailed discussion of the inspections.

"The first will take place at Alpha-7."

Jordan aimed his pointer beam at a satellite image that included a three-state region. Highlighted on the image was a schematic of the 90th Missile Wing's launch facilities and silos. Dodge knew the location of the Minuteman III silos weren't classified. He also knew anyone could use Google to find the same information. As one leg of a triad that included submarine and aircraft-launched intercontinental ballistic missiles, the land-based missiles underscored the basic concept of deterrence. By letting the other guy know you had the power to take him out, you—hopefully—discouraged him from trying to take you out. Still, it gave him a goosey feeling to see those silos so nakedly exposed.

"The inspections will occur in conjunction with scheduled downtime for maintenance," Jordan said. "Ninetieth Missile Wing personnel will conduct the maintenance, supplemented by Boeing personnel as required. Air-force security personnel will secure the site before, during and after each inspection."

Jordan worked his way methodically through slide after slide. Thin and wiry, he clearly showed his former military training in his erect carriage and neatly trimmed mustache. Dodge could only admire his grasp of the most minute details of a treaty that had taken almost a decade to negotiate, debate and push through the legislative bodies of nations.

When the meeting broke up, the Russians gathered their notes and paper copies of the slides. Dodge took Tom Jordan off to the side and advised him of Major Petrovna's strange reaction yesterday. Jordan made a note of it and suggested Dodge apprise the Office of Special Investigations detachment commander, as well.

"Already have."

Dodge turned away, intending to collect his team for the trip out to Alpha-7. The sight of his fellow escort officers reaching for their cold-weather parkas had him swinging back to Jordan.

"One more thing."

"Yes?"

"It's pretty frosty in the mornings. The Russians only brought a couple of small suitcases each. I'm not sure they have any cold-weather gear. I can check the necessary kits out of supply, right?"

"Section five-C-twenty of the protocol covers safety or special equipment," Jordan confirmed. "That includes cold-weather gear."

He'd have Sergeant Lewis detour by supply on the way to the rendezvous point for the convoy out to Alpha-7, Dodge decided. Lieutenant Tate he sent to secure box lunches for their team.

The convoy that would take them to Alpha-7 included a contingent of heavily armed security forces in a lead Jeep and a trailing armored personnel carrier. The convoy wasn't transporting live warheads, but any penetration of an active ICBM silo called for robust security.

Trucks loaded with maintenance personnel and support equipment lined up behind the Jeep. In the center of the convoy was the PT—the payload transporter. A long white boxcar on wheels, it would be angled upright before being rolled over the launch tube. Maintenance crews would then open the blast door that covered the silo, hoist the missile into the PT and perform necessary maintenance to the warheads or guidance systems while shielded from overhead spy satellites. In this case, however, the Russians would be observing the process up close and personal.

The blue bus that would transport the observers to Alpha-7 was waiting with its engine idling. Sergeant Lewis drove up as Dodge and Lieutenant Tate were shepherding their charges onto the bus. Just in time, too. The morning wind hadn't lost its bite. It would be even more bone-cutting out on the plains, with no buildings within a hundred-mile radius to block it.

Lewis joined them in the bus and handed out the parkas. They were designed for wear with military field uniforms. The tiger-striped camouflage jackets were water-resistant, windproof and breathable, with a moisture-wicking barrier for maximum comfort and durability in even the harshest conditions.

The Russian males accepted them gratefully, but Petrovna's blond brows snapped together.

"Why do you give us these? We cannot accept such expensive gifts."

"They're not gifts. They're standard-issue cold-weather gear, covered by section five-C-ten of the inspection protocol."

Her lips pursed, Petrovna treated him to a long stare. The vigorous gust that blasted through the open bus door settled the matter.

"Very well. We will take them. But the section you refer to is five-C-*twenty*."

The convoy rolled out of the staging area a short time later. Luckily, Alpha-7 was only a little over forty minutes from the base. Some of the more remote launch sites required a drive of three or more hours. Being out on the high plains that long when blizzards howled in from the north wasn't fun, Dodge knew from personal experience.

The convoy followed a paved state highway for thirty miles or so before turning off onto one of the dirt-and-gravel roads that bisected the Wyoming countryside. This one ran past miles of fenced-in range dotted with herds of longhorns. A few stunted cottonwoods marked a meandering creek. Tall prairie grasses rippled before the breeze like a sea of football fans doing the wave. Every so often, the helo providing aerial security for the convoy would pass overhead and beat the grass on either side of the road flat.

Each time the chopper swooped by, Dodge's hands twitched. It stuck in his craw to be chugging along on a bus instead of up there, skimming above the hills with the freedom of a hawk.

The convoy finally braked to a stop in the middle of nowhere. Literally nowhere. The plains rolled for miles in every direction, without so much as a barbed-wire fence or tree-lined creek to break their brown monotony. The only sign of human intervention was the slender white radar tower that poked above the next hill.

Engines idling, the long line of vehicles puffed vapor fumes into the cloudless sky while the security-team chief radioed the Missile Alert Facility some fifteen miles distant. The purpose of his call was to advise the MAF that the convoy would be penetrating Alpha-7's outer security zone. He would also pass on a list of personnel entering the launch site for verification by the MAF.

It took some time to complete the personnel checks and deactivate the active and passive sensors guarding the missile's outer field. The security system was so sensitive a passing coyote or antelope could—and often did—trip the sensors. Security forces from Warren responded to hundreds of alarm activations a year, never knowing whether they'd encounter a herd of grazing pronghorn antelope or a wild-eyed terrorist group attempting to infiltrate the site. *That* possibility kept everyone in the missile business on their toes.

After the MAF cleared them for entry, the convoy revved up. A few moments later, the vehicles topped a small rise. Directly ahead lay the fenced-in rectangle that comprised the site. From here, it looked like little more than a flat patch of gravel surrounded by waving prairie grass.

Even when they got closer, the launch site gave little hint of the awesome destructive power lurking just beneath its surface. Aside from the slender white radar tower that received and transmitted data from the security sensors, there wasn't much to see inside the fenced enclosure. A flat manhole cover protected the shaft that allowed personnel access to the silo. A massive concrete slab covered the launch tube itself. Steel doors, laid flat against the gravel, gave access to an underground support building which housed the batteries and support equipment necessary to keep the missile on prolonged strategic alert.

Before allowing anyone into the fenced enclosure, security forces armed with automatic assault weapons positioned themselves around its perimeter. Once they were in place, maintenance personnel backed the payload transporter in and maneuvered it directly over the blast doors.

The bus driver parked just inside the fenced enclosure. Like the maintenance and security vehicles, he kept the bus pointed away from the silo and toward the gate for fast egress if commanded by the distant Missile Alert Facility. Dodge got off the bus first to make sure security set up a rope barrier as required by the protocol. When that was done, the passengers descended.

Their first order of business was to verify the site they were standing on. Captain Tyschenko extracted a GPS locator from his briefcase. The device received signals from GLONASS, the Russian equivalent of the U.S. Global Positioning Satellite System. Originally developed by the military, commercial variations of GPS were now used by everyone from soldiers of fortune to Ford-pickup owners. The Russian team wasted no time verifying and recording the exact coordinates of Alpha-7.

Watching them at work once again stirred the goosey feeling Dodge had experienced during the in-brief. He knew that every U.S. Missile silo was under constant surveillance by spy satellites. He also knew U.S. satellites peered down with the same unwinking vigilance on Russian missile fields. Somehow, that didn't make him feel better about the fact that the Russians were standing right here at ground zero. He remained to one side, saying nothing while his charges finished their preliminary work. After that, there was nothing to do but wait.

"Anyone want coffee?" Sergeant Lewis asked. "This is going to take a while."

He passed around the foam cups he'd obtained from the twenty-gallon boilermaker loaded in one of the trucks. With a word of thanks, Dodge sipped at the steaming brew and watched the activity taking place within the enclosure.

Larissa Petrovna accepted one, as well. Her cheeks pinked from the wind, she sipped at the steaming brew. "Interesting, is it not?"

"And complicated."

"It is not easy, getting into a nuclear-missile silo," the Russian observed drily. "Yours or ours."

"You won't find me complaining about that."

He divided his attention between the Russians and the maintainers positioning the payload transporter over the blast doors. Like a camel hunkering down, the PT's rear end angled down. Then slowly, so slowly, its front end rose until it pointed into the sky.

That done, the maintenance personnel prepared

to descend the shaft that would give them access to the missile itself.

"Watch this," Lewis said as a couple of beefy maintainers wrestled loose the lug nuts on the weather shield covering the shaft. "The minute those guys lift the weather shield, they trigger the inner-zone alarms. The security-team chief has only seconds to enter his codes."

Evidently, the team chief punched in his codes in time. No alarms sounded. No sirens blared. One by one, the maintenance crew disappeared into the shaft.

"There's a second door about twenty feet down," Lewis explained. "They have to unlock more combinations and wait through another sequence of timed delays. Once inside, they'll disconnect the umbilical and hook the hoist to the missile."

Dodge had downed all of his coffee and was working on a refill when several maintenance troops reemerged and initiated the sequence to open the blast door. An ominous rumble echoed like thunder across the site. Slowly, the massive concrete slab rolled out from under the payload transporter. Just as slowly, the hoist raised the upper portion of the Minuteman III into the PT.

Finally, the maintenance-team chief came back and announced they were ready for the observers.

"We have to stay within the roped-off area," Dodge reminded his charges. "And you need to coordinate any pictures with me."

"We know this," Petrovna replied brusquely.

"Yes, ma'am, I'm sure you do."

His boots crunching on gravel, Dodge followed the maintenance-team chief across the site. A moment later, he entered the long, narrow boxcar and came nose to nose with a nuke.

The scheduled maintenance took almost five hours. The sun was dropping out of a sky streaked with flaming reds and gold by the time the convoy reassembled for the return trip.

As interesting as he'd found the entire process, Dodge was glad to head back. There was something real sobering about being up close and personal with a nuclear warhead. He took a couple of steps toward the bus before he noticed Major Petrovna had slowed to a stop a short distance away.

Arms wrapped around her waist, she stared at the jagged peaks of the Rockies. The wind played with a silky, pale gold tendril that had escaped her severe twist. When Dodge moved to stand beside her, he had to fight a ridiculous urge to hook the wayward strand behind her ear.

"These mountains are so beautiful," she murmured. "Taller, I think, than the Caucasus."

"And then some," he agreed.

"My parents would take me to the mountains when I was a girl," she said quietly, as if mesmerized by the glorious scene. "Now I take my Katya, so she may breathe the air. It is so clean, the air of the Caucasus. Like here. Katya could breathe here."

"Does your daughter have respiratory problems?"

The joy she'd taken from the stunning vista faded. He could almost feel her shutting down as she answered slowly, reluctantly.

"The apartment building where we lived… My husband and Katya and I… It took fire."

Dodge knew she was a widow. Knew, as well, that her husband had been killed in a fire. That didn't lessen the impact of her stark recital.

"Katya was then a baby," she said, her gaze on the distant mountains. "She survives the fire, but her lungs are damaged."

"That's tough."

"Da."

The word was little more than a whisper, almost lost in the shiver that wracked the woman from head to toe. Unthinking, Dodge stepped around her, caught the zipper tab of her parka and tugged it up until the high collar came together to frame her face.

Her startled gaze flew up to lock with his. Her eyes were dark pools of blue, her mouth lush and ripe. Little puffs of breath escaped her lips and clouded on the cold air. Dodge thought they came a little faster with each second the two of them stood toe-to-toe. His pulse had sure as hell kicked into a gallop. He was still trying to rein it in when the major took a quick step back.

"It's not…" She stopped, swallowed and dropped her voice by fifty or so degrees. "It's not permitted to touch."

"Yeah, I know."

She turned away, leaving him to deal with the fact that he wanted to kiss her. Badly. And would have, if they hadn't been out in the middle of a windswept plain with a nuclear missile at their backs and a convoy full of personnel looking on. Calling himself ten kinds of a fool, Dodge wrestled the almost overwhelming urge to haul her back into his arms and take a taste of those luscious lips.

The savage urge eased during the long drive back to the base. Some. Dodge made sure to keep his distance while he and his fellow escorts got their charges fed and back to their quarters.

He left Larissa with a brief good-night and made his way across the darkened parking lot. His first task would be to pop a beer, he decided. His second, to call OMEGA and see whether Blade had dug up any additional information on Barlow.

That was the plan, anyway. Right up until three men in dark suits emerged from the shadows outside his door and blocked his way.

Chapter 4

Dodge's reaction to the sudden appearance of three plain-clothed figures blocking his path was as instinctive as it was instantaneous. His muscles bunched, his adrenaline spiked and his senses recorded instantly the age, weight, height and degree of threat emanating from each even before one man detached himself from the others.

"Major Hamilton?"

"Yeah?"

"Sorry to show up on your doorstep unannounced like this."

Dodge knew him now. Paul Handerhand, the

OSI agent he'd contacted last night to report Major Petrovna's odd reaction.

"Operations told us you and the rest of the team had returned from Alpha-7," Handerhand advised. "We've been waiting for you."

"We who?"

"Mind if we go inside for the introductions?"

Nodding, Dodge keyed the door and ushered the three men inside. The older of the two was obviously in charge. He wore an air of authority that sat well with his iron-gray hair and neatly trimmed mustache. Reaching into his suit pocket, he pulled out a black leather ID case.

"I'm Lieutenant Colonel Mike DeWitt, Chief of OSI Counterintelligence for Air Force Global Strike Command. This is Special Agent Ralph Eastbrook, from 20th Air Force."

So Handerhand had called in the big guns. That meant Dodge was now dealing with two additional levels in the chain of command. It also meant his call last night had stirred up a whole bunch of interest within the OSI.

Intros over, DeWitt took the lead. "The folks in Washington were sketchy on your background, Hamilton, but assured me you know your way around highly sensitive cases like this one."

"I've worked a few high-stakes cases," Dodge acknowledged.

"Then you'll understand why we want to talk to you about Hank Barlow." Extracting a microtape recorder, he centered it on the coffee table and hit Record. "Please relate the specific details of the incident that triggered your phone call. What exactly did Barlow say to Major Petrovna?"

"He didn't say anything to her. To either of us, for that matter. He was just passing by, talking to another man."

"About what?"

"The time it would take to develop some specs, I think. I wasn't paying attention."

"But you heard his voice?"

"I heard *a* voice. It was low and gravelly. Like the speaker had something caught in his throat."

"And Major Petrovna reacted to that voice?"

"She did."

"How?"

Dodge hid his annoyance at being asked to reiterate what he'd told Handerhand last night. "She stopped dead in her tracks and turned six shades of pale. When I asked her if she was okay, she spun around and demanded to know if I'd heard him, the man who 'spoke like a dog.' I told her I had."

"What did she say then?"

"She wanted to know who he was."

"And you told her…?"

"I said he was probably a contractor, since the men who passed us were wearing visitor badges."

"But you didn't give her his name?"

"I didn't know his name at the time."

"What did Major Petrovna say then?"

"Not much. Just that she thought she'd heard a voice like that once before, but she'd made a mistake."

"You didn't press her for an explanation?"

"I tried. She said again she'd mistaken the matter and marched down the hall to Colonel Yarboro's office."

"That's it?"

"That's it. Why? What have you got?"

With a glance at the other two men, DeWitt leaned forward and punched the off button. The recorder whirred into silence.

"Henry Philip Barlow is president and CEO of E-Systems, an engineering firm that designs components for commercial satellite-signal translators. Until recently, E-Systems has concentrated its efforts in the civilian sector. With considerable success, I might add. The company's stock soared three years ago when Barlow introduced a new, relatively inexpensive signal translator for GPS data."

GPS? Dodge tensed. In his mind's eye, he could see the wind whipping tendrils of Larissa Petrovna's silvery-blond hair while she and her team received the signals that verified the coordinates of Alpha-7. Was there some connection between the unit the major had held in her hand and Hank Barlow?

"Barlow's company is now expanding its defense-sector work," DeWitt continued. "E-Systems has teamed with two other major subcontractors in a consortium. They plan to bid on the next phase of the National Missile Defense System, which is why Barlow was here a few days ago. Naturally, we're concerned when a chance encounter with a man who might help develop our nation's future defensive systems causes such a marked reaction in a Russian officer."

"Naturally."

"Barlow's made a number of trips to Moscow over the past ten years, primarily on business, most recently as part of a U.S. delegation to look at ways to reduce the trade deficit." Hunching forward, DeWitt planted his elbows on his knees. His eyes were dead serious under his gunmetal-gray brows. "It's entirely possible Major Petrovna met Hank Barlow on one of these trips. We want to know when and where."

So did Dodge. "Why don't you just ask Barlow whether he knows the major?"

"We will if necessary, but I prefer not to tip our hand at this point. One of our agents did pay Barlow a visit at his corporate offices in Denver this morning. Ostensibly, he was there to verify Barlow's travel dates as part of a routine update to his security clearance."

"Did your agent find anything interesting?"

"Nothing related to Major Petrovna or the Russians' visit to F. E. Warren. We're checking with the Defense Intelligence Agency and CIA to see if they've collected any data on Barlow. In the meantime, we'd like you to work your end a little more."

Dodge hiked a brow. "Work my end how?"

"We want you to get a little more friendly with Petrovna than escorts are usually allowed to do. Spend some off-duty time with her, show her the sights. Gain her trust if possible, and find out why she reacted the way she did to his presence."

A wry grin tugged at his lips. Nothing like being given a free pass to do exactly what he'd been thinking about doing during the long drive back to the base.

"She's tough to get close to," he warned, "but I'll do my best."

"From the scuttlebutt circulating down at the 37th helo squadron," DeWitt said drily, "your best is apparently pretty damn good when it comes to women."

When Dodge merely shrugged, the three men rose.

"Get back to Special Agent Handerhand with any information you extract from the major," DeWitt instructed. "I don't have to tell you that this matter is extremely sensitive."

"No, you don't."

The more Dodge thought about it, the more he liked the idea of getting Larissa away from the base. And he couldn't think of any better place to take her than the Double H.

The problem was finding time to do it. Like the missile-launch crews, maintenance worked around the clock, seven days a week. But their schedule depended on a number of variables, not the least of which was the necessity to keep a full complement of missiles on strategic alert. That meant the Russian inspectors adjusted their work hours to that of the 90th Missile Wing's operation.

They didn't get a break in the inspection schedule until three days later. Dodge used the well-deserved hiatus to make his move.

"We're down until Tuesday," he reminded the major when he escorted her to her quarters.

"I know this. It will give me time to update my reports."

"Update them tomorrow night, after we get back."

"Back?" She swung around, frowning. "From where?"

"I thought we would drop in on a working ranch. Give you a chance to see an American cowboy in his natural habitat."

"I have no time for such things."

"Make time. I'll pick you up at oh-nine-hundred."

"Major Hamilton!"

"Nine," he reiterated as the door whooshed shut behind him.

Lara blew out a frustrated breath. Talking to him was like talking to these wild Wyoming winds. She tried most earnestly to maintain a proper distance, to remind herself—and him!—that they must observe strict protocol.

Yet every time she thought she'd hammered the point home, Hamilton would disconcert her. As when he'd turned up her collar. Or insisted on walking her across the darkened parking lot, as though she were no older than Katya. Or smiled at her in the way that crinkled the skin at the corners of his eyes and…

No! She could not allow herself to think such

thoughts. She could not. She was here on a mission vital to both her country and his. More to the point, she would leave in a few weeks.

And yet...

Gathering intelligence was a secondary but critical component of her mission. Like the Americans who had inspected Russia's nuclear arsenal under previous iterations of START, Lara and the others on her team were charged with collecting as much information as they could. Not only about the missiles themselves, but also the personnel who operated, maintained and guarded them.

She could not go to this ranch with Hamilton without clearing the trip with Bugarin, however. She grimaced at the prospect. Later, she decided. She would inform him later. Right now she wanted nothing more than a hot shower and six or seven hours of sleep uninterrupted by the nightmares that had haunted her since she'd arrived at this base.

Dodge had already factored the FSB officer into his thinking. When he called Sam to let him know he was bringing a guest up to the Double H, he also advised that the visit may generate a file on a certain Samuel Hamilton.

"I've been on worse lists," his cousin drawled. "Who's the visitor?"

"Major Petrovna, one of the Russian inspectors."

"I'll put out the welcome mat. What time should I look for you?"

"I'm picking her up at nine. We should be there by ten, ten-thirty."

"Her?"

"Her," Dodge repeated. "But don't get any ideas. The major can ice you with a single glance."

"Well, then, I'll just have to turn up the heat."

Dodge didn't find Sam's laconic comment particularly amusing. He'd witnessed firsthand his cousin's skill at cutting a female out of the herd.

"Keep your hands off the thermostat. If there's any heating to be done, I'll take care of it."

"Hmm. That the way it is, is it?"

"No. Yes. Hell, I don't know. Just dial down your so-called charm."

"I'm not making any promises. See you tomorrow."

Dodge's next call was to OMEGA for an update on Barlow. Blade's digging had turned up some interesting info. Apparently, the man had taken a flyaway baseball bat to the throat during a little-league game as a kid and had to have his voice box reconstructed. He also had a penchant for women.

"Been divorced twice," Blade reported. "Current wife is a twenty-six-year-old blonde, but he's keeping a mistress on the side. He also uses the services of high-priced call girls when traveling. *Very*-high-priced call girls."

"Did he employ any working girls in Moscow?"

"If he did, we can't find a record of it. We'll keep digging. How's it going on your end?"

"Slow, but I'm taking Major Petrovna up to the Double H tomorrow morning. If I can't get her to loosen up there, I'll hand in my badge."

"I might worry about that, if we wore badges."

OMEGA's field-dress unit had outfitted Dodge for missions that required him to play everything from a millionaire jet-setter to a shaved-headed ex-con out for blood. This mission, thank God, had let him slide into more comfortable skin.

He left his air-force uniform hanging in the closet, opting instead for a blue-and-gray flannel shirt, sheepskin vest and a black Stetson, creased exactly the way he liked it.

He crossed the parking lot, still unsure whether Larissa would agree to go with him, but when he rapped on her door she surprised him with the grudging admission that she would like to see some of the countryside he promised.

Like Dodge, she'd dressed comfortably in slacks and her black turtleneck. She'd also released her hair from its habitual tight twist. It flowed over her shoulders like a curtain of pale silk and got Dodge to thinking all kinds of things he damn well shouldn't be thinking.

She said little during the trip. He didn't push her. He'd have plenty of time once they hit the Double H to pump her for information about Barlow. While she gazed out the window at the rolling countryside, he took full advantage of Wyoming's 75-mph speed limit.

Even at that speed, he should have avoided the dusty black SUV that zoomed out of an interstate rest stop. He caught sight of it speeding down the access lane and cut over, but the SUV came on too fast. Its right left fender clipped the Jeep's right bumper and sent it into a spin.

Swearing, Dodge stood on the brakes. All four tires squealed like wounded banshees. The Jeep fishtailed wildly, made two full turns and slammed into a guardrail.

Chapter 5

Sam rolled his pickup to a stop in the parking lot of Converse County's Memorial Hospital Emergency Room. Straight-arming the front door, he made for the desk.

"I got a call from Major Dodge Hamilton. He said they were bringing him here."

"He's in Cubicle Three," the intake tech replied, "but…"

Sam didn't hang around for the buts. He pushed through another set of doors, followed a circular line of curtains to the third cubicle and rattled the curtain aside.

"You got here fast," Dodge commented as the doc

treating him rolled back her stool and snapped off her rubber gloves.

"Fast enough." Sam took in the blood staining his cousin's shirt and bandage decorating his cheekbone. "What happened?"

"Some asshole clipped us coming onto the interstate. Bastard didn't stop, and by the time I got us out of the ditch, he was long gone."

"The son of a bitch better not be from around these parts."

The soft violence in Sam's voice sparked a similar chord in Dodge. He would have a thing or two to say to the SUV's driver when the police tracked him down.

"Did you get a look at the vehicle or any of the tag numbers?"

"I was too busy fighting the wheel."

"Your Russian okay?"

"She seems to be. The doc checked her over and…"

"I take no hurt."

The comment came from the next cubicle. A moment later, the curtain between the two units rolled back. Larissa Petrovna's cool, assessing blue eyes swept over the stranger.

"You are Samuel, I think. The cowboy that

Major Hamilton wishes me to observe in his natural state."

Sam didn't miss a beat. "I would love to show you my natural state, darlin', but my cousin here…"

"That was natural *habitat,*" Dodge drawled.

Obviously confused by the exchange, the major shrugged and held out a hand. "I am Larissa Petrovna. Your cousin has told me something of you."

Sam stretched out a callused hand and enfolded hers. "He's told me something of you, too, Major."

Either his smile or his firm grip must have appealed to the Russian. Head cocked, she almost smiled.

"We are away from the base, no? Ranks are not necessary. I am called Lara for, uh… How do you say it? The nickname?"

"Lara it is."

Well, hell! Here Dodge had spent a whole bunch of hours with this woman and she hadn't offered much more than name, rank and serial number. He was beginning to think he'd made a serious mistake bringing his cousin into the picture. Especially when Sam released her hand with a show of obvious reluctance.

"You're sure you weren't hurt?"

"I was not."

"Too bad." Sam heaved an exaggerated sigh. "I make a helluva nursemaid."

Enough was enough. Dodge pushed off the exam table.

"Looks like we're good to go here, Hoss," he said. "Why don't you bring your truck around while I check us out. Major…" He stopped, shifted, gave her a quick, slashing grin. "Lara, you better come with me. You'll have to sign release forms."

Lara refused to respond to that devilish grin. Or the deliberate use of her name. But a small shiver of delight rippled through her at the sound of it on his tongue.

How he rolled his words, she thought, as they walked the length of the tiled hall. Just as the one called Sam did. It was like music, the way they spoke. Like a zither played by a master—deep and resonant. The melodious sound could not but please her, although the arrogance that often came when this one spoke annoyed her no little bit.

The vending machine at the end of the hall elicited another roll of words, these of considerable relief.

"I don't know 'bout you, but I sure could use some coffee."

"I, too," Lara admitted.

She fished for a dollar from the precious supply in her purse. She'd brought only the bare minimum of cash with her. Any extra she earned from this duty she would send home to Katya. But she needed something hot and strong. The accident had shaken her more than she wanted to admit.

If Hamilton's reflexes had not been so swift, his instincts so sure, she would have been crushed. Then Katya would have only the elderly aunt Lara paid to watch her when duty took her away. The mere thought made her hand shake so that she couldn't extract a bill from her purse.

Reaching past her, Dodge fed coins into the machine. "I'll get this."

"I can pay," she protested through stiff lips.

"I just 'bout got us both creamed. Least I can do is buy you a cup of coffee."

"It is not meet. The treaty protocol…"

"Screw the protocol. How do you like it?"

"With milk and sugar," she conceded. "Much sugar."

He had the hide of a bear, this one. And the charm of a gypsy. She'd seen his like before. They were not unique to America, these too-handsome cowboys. Russia, too, bred her share of careless, cocky rogues. He might wear scuffed boots, the jeans Americans seemed to pull on like a second skin and a wide leather belt with a silver buckle the size of a saucer, but he was the same under the skin as many she'd known in her own country.

Thankfully, her Yuri had been a different sort of man altogether. Solid, dependable, always there for her when she needed him despite the demand of his military duties. He'd been there for Katya, too, when she'd needed him most.

Without warning, Lara's lungs squeezed so swift and hard she had to fight for breath. She stared at the paper cup that dropped into the slot, not seeing the stream of dark liquid that spurted into it. A wall of fire rose between her and the machine. She could almost feel its heat. Smell the acrid smoke it spewed. Hear her baby's cries. Panic twisted inside her like a living thing, ripping her apart, tearing at her soul.

"Here you go, milk and 'much sugar.'"

The flames had lit the night sky. Leaped almost to the stars. And the smoke! So thick and suffocating, it had blinded her.

"Lara?"

She was panting. Trying to draw air into her starved lungs. Screaming inside her head for Yuri, for Katya. Her baby, her tiny, helpless…

"Lara!"

A hard hand gripped her arm, pushed her toward a chair. "You'd better sit down."

She wanted to claw at the tight hold, wanted to

fight free of all restraints, the way she had the night of the fire. The grip was like steel. She couldn't twist away, couldn't…

The floor tilted. The tan-colored walls swam. Choked with panic, Lara saw the coffee cup splash into a trash can. A moment later, she was swept up and crushed against a broad chest. A shout rang out above her head, piercing the panic that beat at her with vicious fists.

"Hey! Doc! We need help here."

Like waves crashing onto a rocky shore, the fear foamed, rose up a final time, receded. She was held fast in strong arms. Cocooned against hard muscles. Safe. The reality pierced her panic, but she was still quaking, still breathing in small, desperate gasps, when Dodge plunged back through the doors to the emergency room.

Someone rushed toward them. A nurse, Lara thought. The doctor followed hard on the attendant's heels.

"What happened?"

"I don't know. We were at the coffee machine and she just started to shake."

"Put her on the exam table."

Voices came at Lara from all directions. The nurse's. The doctor's. Dodge's, deep and rumbling against her ear.

The urge to cling to him jolted through her, sharp and all-consuming. She ached to stay within the circle of his arms. Just for a moment more. Just until the terror buried itself once again in the treacherous past and she'd drawn what she could draw from his strength, his heat.

The violence of her need shocked Lara almost as much as the realization that she'd lost control. Again! For the third time since coming to this country, she'd let the awful memories escape. She hadn't allowed them to surface for years, had never allowed them to take hold of her like that during the day. She'd devoted herself to Katya and her work, pushed Yuri's horrific death as far to the back of her mind as it would go.

It was that voice! The rasping growl that had tripped the safety wires she'd set around her mind. She had to get them set again, had to remember that she was here on an important mission. She couldn't—wouldn't!—let her personal demons jeopardize her career and her country's security.

Fully recovered now and mortified by her lack of control, she sat ramrod straight while the doctor lifted her eyelid and aimed a bright beam at her pupil.

"Keep your eye on the light, please."

Stiffly, without turning her head, she followed the beam. Dodge's face came into view, bruised and tight with concern. No laughter softened the lines of his face. No smile teased his lips. He looked his years now, she thought, and more. Tough. Taut. Worried.

Heat rushed into Lara's cheeks. How ridiculous that she'd clung to him, that she'd *wanted* to cling to him. She hadn't wanted a man since Yuri. Hadn't needed one. Her work kept her busy, and Katya, the joy of her life, filled her heart. She didn't need anything or anyone else. Especially one such as this.

By the time the physician had monitored her blood pressure and pulse rate, Lara was firmly back in control. She would not lose it again. Preempting the doctor, she pronounced her own diagnosis.

"It was the shock, I think, from the accident. It comes late."

"That's definitely a possibility. How do you feel now? Any dizziness?"

"No."

"Do you feel cold or clammy?"

"No."

"Let me see your hands."

She held them out, palms up, relieved to see they didn't tremble. The doctor observed them for a moment, then hooked her stethoscope around her neck and rolled back her stainless-steel stool.

"I think you'll be okay. Just to stay on the safe side,

take it easy for the rest of the day and drink plenty of fluids." Her glance shifted to Dodge. "Looks like you and your friend will be playing nurse, after all. Think you're up to it?"

"We'll manage."

Chapter 6

Lara Petrovna, both Dodge and Sam discovered during the half-hour drive from the hospital to the Double H, didn't take kindly to being coddled. She proved just as stubborn when they walked into the house where Dodge, his two sisters and Sam had spent their boisterous, adventure-filled childhood.

The weathered floorboards creaked a welcome. The comfortable mix of elkhorn table lamps, hand-woven Navajo rugs and worn leather sofas made Dodge feel instantly at home. But when he ordered Lara to plant her butt on one of the whiskey-colored sofas, she declined.

"I am well." Head cocked, she surveyed the bruise

that had blossomed under his bandaged stitches. "Better than you, I think. Should you not take one of those pain pills the doctor prescribed?"

"I don't want to swallow anything that might take me off PRP."

"Ah, yes. Your Personal Reliability Program. It is strict, like ours."

It damn well needed to be. The PRP applied to everyone who worked around or with nukes. The slightest change in lifestyle, family circumstances or medication that might affect a person's physical or mental state had to be reported. Even something as mundane as a cold or allergies that required antihistamines took a person off PRP.

There were no penalties attached to coming off the program, no blame assigned. Everyone associated with nukes wanted the people working beside them to remain fully alert and functioning. Dodge would have to take himself off the program if the pain continued. He was too professional not to.

Before that happened, though, he had a paint-scraped black SUV to track down and a certain Russian major to get close to. At the express orders of the OSI, no less.

More anxious to get to that last task than he should have been, Dodge volunteered his cousin for kitchen duty.

"Why don't you rustle us up some lunch while I give Lara the grand tour?"

Sam hooked a brow but turned a smile on Lara. "How would you like fried potatoes and a fat, sizzling rib eye, homegrown right here on the Double H?"

"I do not know this rib eye," she began doubtfully, "but we eat many potatoes in Russia."

"Not the way I fry 'em up," Sam assured her. "You go on and leave the cooking to me."

"Very well. As long as your cousin does not ask me to wrestle cows or brand them with an iron," she added with a faint hint of a smile.

Damn! Dodge should be prepared by now for the kick to the gut the woman delivered when she thawed even a few degrees.

"No wrestling," he promised. "We tag stock these days, instead of branding them. And we don't run cows, by the way, just feeder steers."

"So you do not breed your cattle, then, but buy them to fatten for market."

He shot her a surprised look. "You know about raising beef, do you?"

"My grandfather came from the Steppes. Horses and cattle were in his blood."

Dodge was impressed. The tough, wiry Cossacks who'd roamed Russia's equivalent to the Great Plains were legendary horsemen.

"Do you ride?" he asked.

"A little."

"Next time you come to visit, we'll get you up on Thunder. Hang loose and I'll grab you a jacket. We wouldn't want you to catch a chill and faint in my arms again, would we?"

To his surprise, a flush stained her cheeks. "No, we would not."

He might have enjoyed her reaction if he hadn't remembered the stark terror that had gripped her there in the hospital. Still, that sudden heat was worth pondering as he made a detour to the bathroom.

His bloodied shirt went into the overflowing hamper. He replaced it with a denim work shirt from the closet where he stashed clothes for his increasingly infrequent visits. He returned to the living room a few moments later with a flannel-lined canvas duster for Lara. Her flush had faded, but she surprised him again when he handed her the duster.

"I do not express the proper gratitude to you, I think. First you get the field jacket for me and the other members of my team. Then you invite me to come with you today." She fingered the buttons on the duster. "I am not always so ungracious, but the treaty protocol is so very strict. One must be careful in circumstances such as ours, no?"

"Very careful. Although I was anything but when that SUV came at us," he added in disgust.

"The accident was no fault of yours," she countered swiftly. "Your quick action saved us both from worse hurt." She cocked her head, studying his face. "You have very sure instincts. You are a good pilot, I think."

"One of the best."

The cocky reply drew another of her rare smiles. "So do all you aviators say."

She was melting fast. So was Dodge, dammit! Reminding himself that he was on a mission here, he held out the duster for her to slip into. She could have wrapped it twice around her thin frame. Patiently, he waited for her to roll up the cuffs.

"All set?"

"Da."

As Dodge walked Lara past the barn to the corral behind it, he tried to assess the pull she exerted on him. It was more than the job. More than the deliberate distance she insisted they had to maintain. She represented such a contradiction in his mind, all cool and remote, with powerful emotions churning just below the surface.

Hooking a boot on the bottom rail of the corral, he treated himself to a long, slow look. She was silhouetted against a late-afternoon sky streaked with gold. Her arms folded on the top rail, she was smiling at the antics of the frisky bay colt one of the mares had dropped this spring.

Just watching her put a hitch in Dodge's breath. Even bundled up in his old duster, she was something. The wind played with her hair and whipped some color into her cheeks. The flush became her, he decided, a delicate rosebud-pink in keeping with her porcelain skin and pale hair. With an itch that wouldn't quit, he wanted to reach over and run his hand through the loose strands. He'd bet it was smoother than spilt milk.

Then there were those scars. Most females would opt for plastic surgery if they could afford it, or try to cover them with makeup if they couldn't. Lara didn't flaunt her tortured flesh any more than she tried to hide it. It was just there, part of her, like her high cheekbones and the hands-off tilt to her chin.

She reminded him of the flowers on a night-blooming cactus, Dodge decided. Pale white blossoms that opened only in the quiet of the night, unseen, unsavored except by those with the patience to wait for them to unfurl, petal by petal, in the moonlight.

He sucked in a swift breath, his mind filled with the sudden image of Lara sprawled across his bed, unfurling for him. His throat went dry, and the hard push against his jeans convinced him he would never figure the woman out. Best to just make his move.

Casually, he reached over to turn up the collar on her borrowed jacket. She started under his hand, every bit as skittish as the bay colt.

"I know, I know," he said, preempting her protest. "It is not permitted to touch."

Her ice-blue eyes narrowed. "Do you mock me?"

"Mock, no. Tease…yes."

The look she gave him could have skinned the bark off a cottonwood in one long peel. Muttering something in Russian, she flattened her palms on his chest and pushed. Obligingly, Dodge retreated a pace or two.

"You are worse than my daughter. She, too, badgers me to get her way."

"Is Katya as beautiful as her mother?"

As before, the mere mention of her daughter's name softened her face.

"No," she murmured, "Katya has more the look of her father."

She'd handed him an opening, such as it was. Fighting a reluctance to delve into a past he knew was painful for her, he probed gently.

"How long were you married?"

She crossed one arm under her breasts. The other

crept up to the underside of her chin. Dodge guessed she had no idea that her fingers trembled when they stroked the tortured flesh.

Cursing himself, he waited for her to work through the memories that seemed to grip her. They weren't happy ones. That much was obvious from the shadows in her eyes when she turned to him.

"Why…why do you ask about my husband?"

"I guess I just wanted to know what makes you who you are," he said softly, realizing at that moment it was true.

She didn't answer, just stared at him with those haunted eyes. Christ! He'd take one of her icy glares any day over that bruised look.

"Lara, I'm sorry."

He couldn't stand the way her fingers trembled against her throat. Advancing the steps he'd retreated a few moments ago, he gathered her into his arms. She got as stiff as an old saddle but didn't push away. She needed comforting, he guessed, as much as he needed to give it.

He held her, just held her, while the wind rustled like brown paper through the cottonwoods planted around the house. The bay colt came to investigate, poking his muzzle through the split-rail fence.

It was a new experience for Dodge, holding a woman, feeling her wind-tossed hair tickle his chin and wanting only to ease her hurts. Wanting *mostly* to ease her hurts, he amended grimly when she shifted in his arms.

"The fire," she said, so low the wind almost snatched the words away. "It…it burned our apartment building to the ground. Yuri saved Katya, but could not save himself."

The pain in her voice stripped him raw. He couldn't exploit it.

"Don't talk about it if it hurts, sweetheart."

The endearment slipped out. Neither of them noticed.

"I think…" Her throat worked. "I think I must. Perhaps by doing so I will chase away the voice in my head. It has haunted me, this voice, since I have come to your country."

Dodge kept perfectly still as she looked away, chasing away her private ghosts. When she turned back, regret flickered deep in her eyes.

"But not to you, Dodge. I cannot speak of these things to you."

Her deliberate withdrawal got halfway down his craw and stuck there. That was the only reason he could come up with for giving in to the insane impulse to reach up and tunnel his fingers through the thick mass of her hair. It was every bit as soft and silky and seductive as he'd imagined.

"Fine," Dodge growled. "Let's not talk at all."

He took full advantage of her startled gasp to tug her close, bend down and cover her mouth with his. She tasted as good as she looked, he decided on a swift rush of heat. Like a swallow from a cold mountain stream on a hot summer day. He drank greedily, and wanted more.

Shifting, he widened his stance and brought her against him. His lips molded to hers. Demanding, coaxing, blackmailing a response. He didn't know whether it was reflex or sheer astonishment that made her mouth open under his, and didn't care.

Long before Dodge was ready, she wrenched away from him. The haunted look was gone, he saw with vicious satisfaction, although the fire that replaced it looked hot enough to boil the hair from his hide. Luckily, he was saved by the bell.

"That's Sam," he said in response to the loud clanging. "Sounds like he's got the steaks on."

Torn between disgust and dismay, Lara stomped toward the house. When had she become so lost to all sense of duty? So weak that she would lean into this cowboy's arms and draw from his strength? And how could she ache to feel his mouth on hers again and again?

She'd yielded to the wild hunger that had leaped

through her at his touch. Just for a moment. Barely long enough for him to shift and gather her closer. Where she'd found the will to wrench out of his hold, she would never know.

Shaken by how much it had cost her to pull away, she said little during a lunch that would normally have fed her and Katya for three days. Her steak was an inch thick and so large it took up three-fourths of her plate. Mounds of potatoes fried with onions and green peppers took up the rest. A bowl of salad sat untouched by the two men in the center of the table. Lara forced down a few bites of the greenery to balance the meat and potatoes but had to admit it was tasteless compared to the succulent steak.

Wielding her fork left-handed in the European manner, she carried a juicy morsel of beef to her mouth with the tines pointed downward. She could only eat a portion of hers but the men cleaned their plates. When they were done, Sam pushed away from the table.

"We have a rule here at the Double H, Lara. One Hamilton does the cooking, the other has to clean up. How about we take the ATVs and I show you some of the high country?"

"I would like this," she replied.

Dodge made what sounded like a low, warning growl deep in his throat. "Sam…"

"We'll see you later, cuz."

Once again, Lara bundled up in the warm duster. Sam insisted she add a hat with a wide brim and a woven leather strap that cinched under her chin. She felt odd in these Western garments. Almost a different person. Perhaps that was why she let herself relax. That, and Sam's so lively charm. He grinned and teased and offered her such outrageous compliments as they made their way to the barn, that she could only shake her head in amusement.

Once inside the barn, he opened a stall door and whisked canvas covers off two vehicles with monster, tractor-type wheels. "These are Yamaha Grizzly 700s. They're as powerful as they are big. You sure you can handle one?"

Lara had to laugh. "I've launched test SS-18s. I think I can manage this little toy."

They crossed the meadow beyond the barn and took a trail that soon had them climbing into the mountains. Sam drove with care, slowing several times to navigate around fallen logs. Lara followed his lead while her mind's eye recorded every detail of their journey. She'd never seen such glorious color. The white birches reminded her of home, but the blazing red of what Sam called serviceberry trees enchanted her. As did a stand of aspen. The song of the wind rustling through their shimmering gold leaves brought a contentment that flowed through Lara like fine, mulled wine.

That sense of peace diminished as they returned to a ranch house bathed in the shadows of the high peaks. To Lara's disgust, an insidious, irrepressible tingle of anticipation licked at her veins. As much as she'd enjoyed Sam's company, it was Dodge who stirred sensations that she could not, *would* not allow free rein. Consequently, she kept her smile cool and her responses polite when he asked how she'd enjoyed the ride.

"Very much. Now, I think, we must return to the base."

"It's still early," Sam protested. "You should stay for dinner. Better yet, stay the night."

"We cannot."

Dodge countered with a shrug. "Actually, we can. We've got another two days' downtime."

"It's…" Despite herself, Lara couldn't meet his gaze. "It's impossible."

"Why?"

He knew why. She had only to hear how he rolled the question so slowly, so deliberately, to know he challenged her. No, dared her.

"It is impossible. I'm sorry, but I must ask one of you to drive me back to Cheyenne."

Her flat tone said the matter was closed. Sam, apparently, was as deaf as his cousin.

"If Dodge says you're off for a few days, there's no reason to rush back."

"There is every reason. I brought no clothes, no tooth powder..."

"Tooth powder we can handle. And my sister leaves some things here for when she comes up with the kids. I think we can outfit you for a day or two."

"Perhaps you do not understand," Lara said carefully. "I will have to make a report of my visit when I return."

"To the FSB officer on her team," Dodge explained.

She wasn't surprised that his cousin grasped immediately what the initials stood for. The FSB was almost as well-known around the world as the CIA.

"So you file your report," Sam said with a shrug. "It's no skin off my nose if my name turns up on a file in Moscow."

Oh, for...

Exasperated, Lara started to insist. A belated realization stilled the stern order she was about to issue.

Dodge must know why she'd accepted his invitation in the first place, just as she was well aware of the subtle motivation behind it. He, like she, hoped to milk as much information as possible from his counterpart.

Was that why he'd kissed her? she thought with a sudden, sinking feeling. To entice her into lowering her guard so she would reveal more than she should? If so, he'd come perilously close to succeeding. For a reckless moment, she'd wanted nothing more than to give in to the wild hunger the man stirred in her.

The realization was both sobering and steadying. Now that she'd put that kiss in a rational framework, she could deal with it. And with Dodge. Or so she assured herself as she accepted Sam's invitation with only half-feigned reluctance.

"I could remain until tomorrow, if you are sure it will not cause you inconvenience."

"It won't," he assured her.

"Then I thank you for the invitation."

"You're welcome. You can use the spare bedroom." His grin slipped out. "Unless you'd like to share mine."

Dodge's breath hissed in, but Lara had his cousin's measure now. Laughing, she shook her head.

"No, I do not wish to share your bed. Nor should you make such suggestions. They are, how do you say? Not approximate."

"Appropriate," he corrected.

"Don't worry," Dodge said with no touch of amusement in his voice. "I'll make sure this ugly horse's patoot behaves himself."

But would *he?* Lara found herself wondering as afternoon faded to evening. Supper was an easy affair of stew topped with doughy biscuits, then the Hamiltons endeavored to teach her a game called Texas Hold 'Em. She was about to lose the last of the pennies Sam had supplied from a big glass jar when Dodge's cell phone rang. He excused himself to take the call in another room and returned with the news that the Wyoming Highway Patrol had found a black SUV abandoned some fifty miles west of Douglas.

"It was reported stolen last night," he relayed. "The dents and paint scrapings make it a pretty safe bet it's the same vehicle that sideswiped us. It was also wiped clean."

"Wiped clean?" Lara echoed. "What does this mean?"

"It means whoever stole it made care to leave no fingerprints that could identify him."

Lara was no stranger to stolen vehicles or daring thieves. The black market in Russia defied all official attempts to suppress it. Apparently it thrived here in America, as well. At this point, however, she was too tired to worry about such things. The brisk mountain air and surfeit of food had robbed her of energy.

They had also submerged, temporarily at least, the memories that had haunted her these past days. After reiterating that she must return to base in the morning, she settled between clean-smelling sheets and fell into a deep, dreamless sleep.

Chapter 7

Lara flatly refused to remain at the Double H a second day. Sam tried to convince her otherwise, but she held firm. Grumbling, he brought his pickup around to the front of the house shortly after breakfast. She wedged into the front seat between him and his cousin for the ride into Douglas, where Dodge had arranged another rental.

Lara said goodbye to Sam with the wind swirling dried cottonwood leaves around her legs and the sky an ominous gray. The sun had disappeared behind dark clouds that now piled one on top of another. Dodge lifted his face and scanned the horizon.

To her disgust, Lara felt her stomach kick at the

sight of him testing the weight of the air against his tanned, weathered skin. He wore the clothes he'd changed into after the accident yesterday. Jeans, denim shirt, down vest, the well-creased black cowboy hat parodied in so many films of the American West. On him, the clothes looked right.

As right as his military uniform.

Lara didn't need the reminder of who he was— who *she* was—but it hit hard anyway. So hard that she nodded grimly when he said they'd better get going.

"Sky's going to open up," he warned. "Feels more like rain than snow, but you never know this time of year."

The deluge hit only a few miles south of Douglas. Lara couldn't but be thankful for the diversion. It forced Dodge to keep his attention on the road, leaving her to spend the rest of the trip listening to rain drum against the pickup's roof and preparing for what she would face when she returned to the base. It would not be pleasant.

She would have to report the accident yesterday to Aleksei Bugarin. She needed to report as well the rasping voice she'd heard—and the agonizing memories it had evoked.

She dreaded having to speak of Yuri and the night

of the fire with Bugarin though. The FSB officer was a pig. There was no other word for him. He gobbled his food like a swine at the slops, swilled vodka until he was blind most nights and had more than once suggested they could make their stay in the United States far more enjoyable by sharing a bed.

Yet Lara had to tell him. She couldn't jeopardize her mission, couldn't risk letting the memories of that awful night cloud her judgment. What she did here was too vital to her country's future. After a decade of slashed budgets, fractured commands and black marketeering of everything from boots to antimissile defense systems, the military was a hollow shell, barely able to provide an adequate shield for the motherland.

That was just one of the reasons Lara believed so passionately in the START treaty. The only way to ensure Russia's ability to protect itself against the United States—the one nation on earth that had demonstrated its willingness to loose the devastation of atomic weapons—was to reduce the U.S. nuclear arsenal. If that meant reducing Russia's arsenal at the same time, so be it.

Closer to home, the very real possibility of dissidents gaining control of the strategic missiles located in their regions often put her and her comrades in the Russian strike force into a cold sweat. With each step in the elimination of nuclear warheads, Lara felt that much closer to securing a future for Katya.

She couldn't let anything interfere with that process.

Anything!

The rain was still coming down when they topped a rise and Cheyenne emerged from the natural hollow cut by Crow Creek. The elevation gave Lara a bird's-eye view of the city that had sprung up along the banks of the creek.

The streets were laid out in a precise grid, with the round-domed capitol in the center and a scatter of tall buildings running north and south. Iron tracks threaded through the vast railroad yard on the south side of the city, then cut east and west through the plains surrounding Cheyenne on all sides.

The city reflected the character of its population, Lara thought. Tough and tenacious. Stubbornly isolated, far from the centers of population they supported with their vast cattle ranches and fields of wheat. Proud of their independence and their unplaned edges.

Much like the man who sat beside her. Too close beside her.

Despite her determination to remember that they straddled opposite sides of a very dangerous fence, she'd scarcely drawn a full breath during the drive. It worried her, this absurd awareness of the American. With a career spent working almost exclusively with men, she should not be so affected by a sun-weathered face and a body characterized by lean hips, flat belly and sinewy muscles. Especially when they came packaged with such irritating arrogance.

Not that he'd displayed such arrogance when he'd held her in his arms yesterday afternoon. He'd been so gentle, she recalled with a flush of mortification. So comforting. She, who prided herself on her strength of will and ability to function with icy precision in any crisis, had snatched at the comfort he offered.

And that kiss. How could she have allowed it?

She still couldn't believe how the feel of his mouth on hers had stirred such swift and fierce hunger. She'd had no man since Yuri. Wanted no man since Yuri. Katya and her military duties filled her life.

She had to put all thoughts of Dodge Hamilton out of her head. Had to focus on her mission. Only her mission. Jaw set, she barely waited for him to pull to a stop outside the Visiting Officers Quarters before she shouldered open the door. The icy drizzle needled her face and reminded her she still wore the flannel-lined duster he'd loaned her yesterday.

She popped the top buttons and started to remove it. "I thank you for the loan of this coat."

Before she could shrug out of its warm folds, he took her elbow and steered her toward the building.

"Why don't we do this inside, out of the rain?"

Lara's lips thinned. He put his hands on her too easily, this one. Far too easily. She must end that habit. They would go inside. She would thank him coolly for the visit to his home. Then she would inform him that they must now resume their respective roles.

After which she would find Bugarin. The prospect tightened her throat.

The outer doors swung shut behind them, cutting out the rain and encasing them both in the dimness of the hall. Lara led the way down the corridor and inserted her key in the door to her suite. When the door swung open, she turned to Dodge with a fixed smile.

"I thank you for a most interesting visit."

"You're welcome."

She tried once more to remove the warm jacket. Once again, he stopped her.

"Keep it."

"No, I cannot. I…"

Dodge trapped the rest of her protest in her throat. Trapped Lara, too, in a shock of surprise. She stood frozen while rain dripped from his hat brim onto her cheeks and his mouth moved over hers with a sensuality that demanded a response.

She ached to give it. Her treacherous body flared with instant hunger, even as determination iced her veins. She refused to afford him the satisfaction of jerking her head away, refused to show by so much as a blink how much he'd angered her when at last he raised his head.

"You will not kiss me again. Ever."

She kept her voice cold and flat and devoid of all inflection, as though such behavior did not merit excess emotion. Any of the junior officers who worked under Lara would have blanched at such a tone and stammered an immediate acknowledgment. Hamilton merely shoved his hat back on his head and regarded her with a rueful glint in whiskey-colored eyes.

"I can't guarantee the 'ever' part, but…"

"There are no buts. You must remember who you are, and who I am."

"I do, sweetheart. Believe me, I do."

"Nor can you address me so. From this moment, we are once again Major Petrovna and Major Hamilton."

"Yeah, well, we'll see."

He tipped two fingers to his brim and left Lara once again prey to wild emotions. Damn the man! He roused her to such fury and such heat. Racked by both, she turned toward her door and inserted the key.

A sound from the other end of the hall brought her head whipping around. Her heart thumped painfully against her ribs as she stared at the man standing in an open door at the far end of the corridor.

Bugarin eyed Dodge's retreating back for several moments before he emerged from his own room, closed the door behind him and sauntered down the hall. Lara's heart sank at the glint in his dark eyes. It reminded her all too forcefully of the lizards that flattened themselves on rocks along the shores of the Black Sea.

"That was quite an interesting scene, Larissa Petrovna."

"Do you think so?"

Baring his teeth in a smile that raised the hairs on the back of her neck, he pushed past her. She closed the door behind her and clenched her jaw as he lowered his bulk into the armchair.

"Tell me," he purred, steepling his fingers on his paunch, "did you seduce Hamilton last night, or he you?"

It would not do to show fear. Like the carrion they were, Aleksei Bugarin and his kind fed off others' weaknesses.

"Neither." She managed a credible shrug. "I did, however, allow him some familiarities…as you saw."

"Yes, I did."

He was enjoying this, she knew. The little bastard thought he'd found something he could hold over her head. He would try to make her sweat before he finished with her.

"How strange…and how unlike you, Larissa Petrovna." He propped his pudgy chin on his finger-tips and let his glance roam the length of her body. "You have not used your undeniable attractions to extract information before."

"Nor did I this time."

"Ahhh. So what do I report? It was lust, not duty, that took you into the arms of an American officer?"

"Report what you will." She feigned total disinterest. "But at least be accurate. I did not go into his arms."

An unhealthy purple rose in the FSB officer's veined cheeks. Pushing out of the chair, he stalked across the room.

"Nor did you slap his face," he ground out, "as you slapped mine."

His breath fouled the air between them. Although it was not yet noon, he'd been drinking. Heavily. Making no attempt to hide her scorn, Lara raked him with a withering glance.

"He didn't maul me, Aleksei, as you did. And you

were lucky I only slapped you. Had I not exercised rigid restraint that day, you would now be walking with a permanent limp."

Bugarin glared at her through the haze left by the vodka. Damn the woman! Somehow she'd turned the tables on him yet again. Who was she to act so cold, so superior? She'd treated him like one of her lieutenants since the start of this cursed trip. He didn't answer to her, only to his superiors in the FSB.

He hated them, these self-righteous military officers he was assigned to watch. They mouthed terms like *honor* and *courage* and *duty* to the motherland, yet most would sell the uniforms off their troops' backs if offered the right price.

Those who *didn't* rake in extra rubles from the black market were even worse. They actually believed they could survive without compromise. Larissa Petrovna was such a one. The stupid bitch would break before she would bend. And Aleksei would thoroughly enjoy watching her snap.

"You dare to speak of endangering our mission?" he shot back. "You, who spends the night in a house that has not been checked for listening devices or hidden cameras?"

"I told you where I was going before I left," she reminded him icily. "You raised no objection."

"You told me you would be back by nightfall."

"The accident left us without a vehicle."

"This accident occurred yesterday morning. You had plenty of time to arrange transportation back to the base, had you wished to."

She had no answer for that. Bugarin pressed his point home with a vicious thrust.

"Hamilton must have been quite persuasive, to keep you the whole night at his house. What secrets did you tell him, Larissa Petrovna, while he rode you?"

"I will say this again, just once. He did not ride me. Nor did I tell him secrets."

Vodka may have slowed his thought processes, but Aleksei had served too long with the FSB for drink to dull his instincts.

Larissa's glance didn't waver. Scorn still sharpened her voice. Yet he knew at once she'd lied. Or perhaps withheld a part of the truth. The two were the same in his mind.

"But you told him something," he murmured with a satisfied smile. "Something you must now tell me."

"Yes."

A feral excitement curled in his belly. It was like sex, this sudden jolt he got whenever he uncovered that which others wanted to keep hidden. The intensity of it burned the fumes from his brain and restored his heady sense of power.

He could have laughed at the look on her face. She detested him, and must now open herself to him. Depending on what she revealed, he might well be able to use it to force her to open in other ways, too.

His groin tightened in delighted anticipation. He could see her, flat on her back, those slender white thighs spread wide. He would make her lie there, just lie there, unmoving, while he played with her. Then he would roll her over, put her on her knees and take her like the bitch that she was.

Bugarin's triumph showed clearly on his face, sickening Lara. He would wield the club she was about to hand him with glee. She knew it as well as she knew her own child's cry in the night.

A craven impulse to keep silent raced through her. What if she didn't tell Bugarin about the voice? What if she just put it out of her head, forced the memories back to the darkest recesses of her being, where they had hidden until a week ago?

No! She could not do that to Yuri. To herself.

She slanted another look at the FSB officer's red, wet lips. A shudder rippled down her spine. Slowly, from the wasteland of her heart, she dragged out the truth.

"The day we arrived here, I heard a man speaking with an odd voice. One I have heard before, in Moscow."

Whatever Bugarin had expected, it obviously wasn't that. He stared at her stupidly. "What man? Who is he?"

"I don't know. His was just one voice in a crowd of many who passed by. By the time I recovered from my shock, he was gone."

Frowning, the FSB officer struggled to sort through her tale. "What was so odd about this voice?"

"It is most distinctive. Deep, like a frog's, and rasping." Her chest tightened. "It was also the voice I heard just before the fire at my apartment building six years ago."

"What fire? Ah!" His gaze sharpened, slid to her throat. "The one that killed your husband?"

"Yes."

With a callousness that took her breath away, he shrugged aside the horror of Yuri's death. That was *her* nightmare, not his. His only interest lay in the puzzle she'd just presented him.

"What was he doing in your apartment building, this mysterious speaker?"

"Arguing with the woman who lived next door. I heard only a few words when I passed by her door.

He called her a whore. She laughed, then cried out to him to not be so rough, not to hurt her."

"She screamed?"

"No, there was no scream."

Only the one small cry. Not frightened, really. No touch of panic, or Lara would have stopped and pounded on the door. She'd paused, listened for a moment, then gone on her way. A lover's spat, she remembered thinking.

Bugarin came to much the same conclusion. His lip curled in a sadistic smile.

"She must have liked it, then, the rough way he used her."

He contemplated the scene Lara had evoked in his dirty little mind for so long, she had to bite the inside of her lip to hide her revulsion.

"She was Russian, this woman?"

"Yes. I did not know her well. She'd moved in only the week before. She died that night."

"In the fire?"

"Yes."

She would not tremble, would not let her voice quaver. At the first sign of weakness, he would pounce on her like a vulture on a rotting carcass.

"How am I to understand this?" he demanded caustically. "You heard a voice six years ago, but you don't know whose. You think you heard it again last week, but didn't bother to report the matter to me."

"I'm reporting it now."

"You're a bit late, Larissa Petrovna."

She endured the sneer, realizing he didn't know what to make of the information she'd just given him any more than she did.

"I'll send a query to my department head," he said finally. "Perhaps we have a file on someone with a voice like a frog's, or on this woman who lived next door to you. Give me her name."

"Elena Dimitri."

He jotted down the few pitiful details Lara could provide. She'd only seen the woman once or twice, in the hallway. Young and quite attractive, she'd smiled cheerfully in passing but kept to herself. A week after moving in she was dead, her body burned beyond recognition.

Like Yuri's.

The door slammed behind Bugarin a few moments later. Blindly, Lara crossed her arms and stared at the rain painting the window in shades of gray. One hand reached up to tremble against the side of her throat.

She had no idea how long she stood there before she noticed the odd pattern of the rain rivulets.

Across the parking lot, Dodge paced the confines of his living room. The gray skies and icy drizzle had him feeling caged and restless and totally frustrated.

Aw, hell! Who was he kidding? It wasn't the weather that had him tied up in knots. It was a certain blue-eyed major.

He was damned if he could rationalize kissing her. Not once, but twice. He knew how dangerous it was to mix business with pleasure. Especially in his kind of business.

He'd also been burned once, badly. True, he'd been young and stupid enough to confuse lust with love. Also true, he'd refused to recognize the signs that she'd tired of him until he came home to find her gone. He'd done a damned good job since that humiliating experience of keeping his relationships with women loose and easy.

Not that he could claim anything resembling a relationship with Lara Petrovna. In addition to the fact that she was a Russian *and* a missile officer *and* his target, she was as prickly as a cactus. Yet her barriers had slipped enough for him to glimpse the woman behind them, and she pulled at him like none other had in longer than he could remember.

So now he'd opened a door he was finding damned hard to shut. Added to that, this business with Hank Barlow was eating into his gut. Almost as much as being sideswiped by a stolen SUV. From all appearances, the two incidents were unrelated but Dodge couldn't shake the suspicion they fit in some way. He was still trying to jam the pieces of the puzzle together when the phone in his quarters rang some hours later.

"Hamilton."

"This is Sergeant Rafferty at the wing command post, sir. Colonel Yarboro wants you to report to Major Petrovna's quarters immediately."

Dodge's glance whipped to the window. Although the rain had fogged the panes, he could see her building clearly. See, too, the vehicle that came screeching to a halt just outside it. Paul Handerhand of the OSI jumped out, while another vehicle with the distinct markings of the security forces pulled up behind Handerhand's.

Dodge's gut twisted. The sudden, all-consuming fear that something had happened to Lara had him slamming the phone down and racing for the door.

The wing commander's white-topped vehicle arrived as Dodge sprinted across the parking lot. Colonel Yarboro emerged, wearing jeans, a leather jacket and a look that signaled imminent danger to life and limb for anyone who crossed him. Tom Jordan, the wing's START officer, scrambled from the passenger seat.

"Aleksei Bugarin has filed an official protest," Yarboro announced without preamble.

The terse announcement brought a low hiss from Special Agent Handerhand. Dodge barely managed to smother a curse.

Christ! Had Bugarin seen him corner Lara in the hall? Or had she felt obligated to report the kisses Dodge had laid on her? He couldn't bring himself to believe that, but he squared his shoulders and prepared to admit that he'd had his hands all over her.

He didn't get the chance. Yarboro continued in a tone as cold and cutting as the drizzle. "Bugarin sent the protest to the Russian Embassy. From there, it went to Moscow and came back to the U.S. through diplomatic channels to the Defense Threat Reduction Agency. DTRA passed it to the Department of Defense. I just received it."

The colonel's flinty gaze cut from Dodge to Handerhand and back again.

"We stand accused of violating section two-seven-B of the inspection protocol."

Dodge didn't even try to pretend he knew the reference. "By doing what, sir?"

"By installing an unauthorized listening device in Major Petrovna's quarters."

Chapter 8

"A bug?" Dodge echoed grimly. "You're saying someone planted a bug in Lara's room?"

"I'm not," Yarboro snapped, "the Russians are." Making no effort to hide his extreme displeasure at this turn of events, he turned to the treaty-compliance officer. "Tom, you want to let them know we're here, so they can show us this device?"

Jordan didn't have to let them know. Bugarin must have been watching for Yarboro's arrival. The FSB officer bustled out of the building with his collar turned up against the drizzle. Lara exited a few steps behind him. Her face was ashen, and she met Dodge's look with an icy one of her own.

He got the message. The listening device—if there was one—had violated more than treaty protocol. It had shattered whatever fragile trust Lara might have had in him or in any Americans.

"It is here."

Huffing, Bugarin led the way not into the building, but alongside it. He counted the windows, stopped outside Lara's and stepped over the boxwoods planted beneath. Mulch squished under his boots as he pointed to the upper windowpane.

"There."

Even with Bugarin pointing directly at it, the flat dime-size device was almost impossible to see. It was made of a clear, hair-thin plastic. The tiny fiber inside had a transparent coating. Dodge suspected the device never would have been discovered if not for the rivulets of rain curving delicately around its outer edges.

"I have scanned it with my equipment," Bugarin informed them. "It is most definitely a listening device, and as such, a violation of the treaty protocol. I must demand to know when it was placed and by whom, so I may include that information in the report I send to my superiors."

"I want to know a few things myself." Yarboro's low, lethal reply made the FSB officer back up a step and shed some of his self-righteous indignation. "Is this the only device you've found?"

"Da."

"No others, in any of the rest of the rooms?"

"Nyet."

"Then you won't object if I have my people do a double check." The colonel swung to his OSI detachment commander. "I want the best you've got on this, Handerhand. Have them scan every window, every exterior door, every crack in the wall."

"Yes, sir."

The colonel threw another glance at the rain-soaked window, blew out a disgusted breath and crooked a finger.

"Come with me, Hamilton."

Dodge followed him to his staff car and braced for what he knew was coming. Sure enough, Yarboro waited only to make sure they were out of hearing before letting loose with both barrels.

"I'd better not learn you and that hush-hush outfit you work for in D.C. are behind this."

"We're not, sir."

"You sure about that?"

"I'm sure."

"Then who the hell is?"

"I don't know."

Yaroboro's eyes narrowed to slits. "But you've got a theory?"

"More of a hunch than a theory."

"Let's hear it."

"I'm thinking that little bit of plastic is how the driver of a black SUV knew Major Petrovna and I would be cruising a deserted stretch of I-25 yesterday morning."

Dodge felt a sudden kick low in his belly as several of the pieces of the puzzle he'd been trying to force-fit suddenly came together.

"I'm also thinking the bug might not have anything to do with the START treaty and a whole lot to do with Lara. I need to check the date of the fire that killed her husband, sir. I also need to have our people analyze the components of the device. I'll get with Handerhand and have it couriered to the wizard who heads OMEGA's electronics division. I'm betting it'll take her and her folks all of five minutes to tell us if any of its components were designed or manufactured by E-Systems' Communications Division."

"Hell! You think Hank Barlow's behind this?"

"It's still conjecture at this point."

Conjecture, maybe, but backed by gut instinct. It was time he paid a personal visit to the CEO of E-Systems, Dodge decided. First, though, he needed to set things straight with Lara.

He strode back to where she stood a little way apart from her FSB counterpart, who was observing and documenting the removal of the bug. Shoulders hunched against the cold, she knifed Dodge with a look that could have bent steel, then turned her attention back to the others.

"We didn't plant that device."

"We?" She gave a huff of scorn. "You speak for your entire government, then?"

"Pretty much."

"You, a mere major?"

This wasn't the time to tell her that he worked for an agency other than the Department of Defense.

"Listen, Lara, I can't prove it—yet—but this bug may trace back to Hank Barlow."

He watched closely for a reaction. A flicker of her eyes, maybe. Or a slight flare of her nostrils. But she gave no indication the name meant anything to her.

"Who is this Barlow?"

"The man whose voice you heard here…and in Moscow the night your husband died."

There was no denying the reaction this time. Shock drained what little color the cold hadn't already taken. The puckered scars stretched tight across the underside of her jaw.

Something pulled inside Dodge, sharp and hard, like a muscle cramp in his chest. He ached to kiss that tortured skin, to stroke her cheek and throat until her eyes burned with another sort of fever. Instead, he steeled himself against the horror he'd evoked.

"You know who he is?" she whispered.

"Yes. But I don't know what really happened the night of the fire. You need to tell me, Lara. You need to trust me."

Her glance whipped to the FSB officer. She was caught between them, Dodge knew. Damned if she did, damned if she didn't.

"I cannot…"

"You have to," he countered brutally. "Otherwise the inspection gets scrubbed, you and your team go home, a treaty that's taken a decade to push through falls apart and both our countries go back to pointing an unlimited number of missiles at each other's throat."

Her back stiffened. Her chin came up. As Dodge had anticipated, the officer in Lara Petrovna wouldn't allow the woman to jeopardize her mission.

"I must speak with Bugarin, tell him what you know and get his permission to, how do you say? Pump you for more information."

Her inflection didn't change. Nor did her tight expression. But Dodge didn't miss the distaste that flickered in her eyes for the cat-and-mouse game they were both forced to play.

"I will come to your quarters later," she told him stiffly. "When the business here is finished."

Finishing it took some time. Since the device was discovered on a U.S. base, the military took charge of it. Bugarin insisted on photographing and documenting its removal, then peered over the shoulders of the OSI counterintelligence techs who swept the quarters of the other Russian team members. Dodge used the interval to contact Blade and arrange immediate transport of the wafer-thin disk peeled off Lara's window to OMEGA headquarters.

"Mac's gonna love this," Blade commented.

"Yeah, I know."

Mac, aka Mackenzie Blair Jensen, had served as OMEGA's guru of all things electronic for years. After the birth of her twins, she'd assumed more of a consultant role. Nick Jensen had already announced that he intended to do the same after the next presidential election. Dodge was profoundly glad both Lightning and his genius of a wife were still available for this one, though.

"Tell Mac that I need her analysis ASAP," he advised Blade. "My gut says this train's moving down some fast tracks."

"Roger that."

He had the device on an air-force jet and en route

to Washington in less than a half hour. Then he returned to his quarters to wait for Lara.

Dodge had mastered the fine art of patience over the years. First as a kid, when his dad had taught him and Sam to hunt game with slow stealth. Then as a teen, when he'd learned to wait precious seconds for an open receiver instead of recklessly lobbing a football downfield. Again and again as an adult, both in the military and in his missions for OMEGA. Stalking human prey took even more tenacity and patience.

So he had no excuse for his reaction when Lara rapped on his door an hour later. He closed it behind her, hooked her elbow and spun her into his arms. No excuse, that is, other than her pallor and the bruised, haunted look in her eyes.

That disappeared fast enough when she flashed him a look of utter disbelief. "Are you mad!"

"I must be," he admitted wryly. "With everything else going down, all I could think of this past hour was getting you in my arms."

Not at all impressed by his admission, she treated him to a stare that would have sent a lesser man running for the door. "This is a dangerous game you play, Dodge Hamilton."

"Not that it matters, sweetheart, but I'm long past the play stage."

His gaze roamed her face, lingering on those brilliant blue eyes, the high cheekbones, the mouth he ached to kiss. The individual features were etched on his mind. The woman they comprised, Dodge now suspected, was etched on his heart.

He couldn't have picked a worse time or place for this. There was too much at stake, too many issues unresolved. Yet he couldn't hold back a husky confession.

"Every time I touch you, Larissa Petrovna, I want you more."

He expected her to shove out of his arms and deliver a withering broadside. Instead she let out a shuddering breath.

"I want, as well."

Dodge savored a fierce satisfaction at the admission for all of two seconds. Then she tilted her chin and blasted his masculine ego all to hell.

"I want to know if this man you spoke of caused the death of my husband and the pain my daughter still suffers. If I must sleep with you to make this happen, I will sleep with you."

Shock rocked him back on his heels. Fury followed hard in its wake.

"You don't have to sleep with me to make anything

happen. I'm going to stay on this business with Barlow whether or not we get naked."

"Oh?" Her lip curled. "And you were not thinking to, as you say, get naked when you opened the door to me?"

"No. Yes. Oh, hell!" With another vicious curse, he reined in his anger and fumbled for the truth. "I desire you, Larissa Petrovna. In ways I don't begin to understand. You fascinate me and challenge me and make me ache to kiss away the lines of strain that mar your face."

"It is not strain that mars my face," she countered bitterly. "It is the past."

"The past," he agreed, "and the present. I see the worry here, beside your mouth."

Lara stood stiff as a fence post while his thumb traced a light pattern at the corner of her mouth.

"And here, around your eyes."

She refused to respond, refused to acknowledge the tiny ripples his thumb caused just under her skin. She couldn't deny the hunger his touch roused, however. It curled and coiled and came alive within her, stirring desperate thoughts.

Why not give him what he wanted? What *she* wanted? He promised sex in its most primitive, cleansing form. He would drive into her. Strong and healthy and eager as a stallion, he would fill her and force every thought, every fear out of her mind. Lara needed that oblivion. She *craved* that oblivion.

"I will not lie," she whispered, driven to the truth. "I want your hands on me. I want your body on mine. In mine."

He sucked in a swift breath, but before he could pounce like a hungry bear on her admission, Lara pleaded with him.

"First tell me about this man you spoke of earlier."

He let out the breath he'd drawn in and nodded. "I made some coffee. You sit, I'll pour us a cup and we'll talk."

It took Dodge only long enough to lace a mug of heavily sugared coffee with milk to make a command decision. Given the number of civilian and military agencies involved in this operation, he probably should clear the release of the information they'd gathered on Barlow to the Russians. But he couldn't ask Lara to trust him if he wasn't willing to do the same.

When he returned, she took the mug and closed her hands around it but didn't drink. Her whole being remained focused intently on him while he gave shape and substance to the voice he knew had come to haunt her dreams.

"His name is Henry William Barlow. He got hit in the throat in a freak accident when he was a kid and had to have his voice box reconstructed. Ever since, he's spoken with that rasp you heard."

She absorbed that without blinking an eye.

"At twenty-six, Barlow started a company called E-Systems. Five years later it was a multimillion-dollar operation. Ten years after that, the U.S. Secretary of the Treasury appointed him to an international trade commission."

Her knuckles whitened on the mug. She'd guessed what was coming.

"As a member of the commission," Dodge continued slowly, "Barlow traveled extensively in Europe and the Far East."

"And Russia?" she whispered. "He came to Russia?"

"Yes."

"When?"

"He's made a number of trips."

Her throat worked. Her eyes lit with blue fire. "One was in June. June of six years ago. He was in Moscow on the sixteenth day of the month."

She wasn't asking. She knew it in her bones, just as Dodge knew she was right.

"Is that the day of the fire?" he asked quietly.

"Da."

"I'll confirm that. But let's assume he was there. What was he doing in your apartment building?"

Carefully, very carefully, she set aside the coffee mug. Dodge suspected she was using the few seconds to decide whether to leap the same chasm he had.

Would she trust him? Could she? He didn't have a clue until she lifted her eyes to his.

"Barlow comes to see a woman named Elena Dimitri. Her apartment is on the same floor as mine."

Elena Dimitri. Dodge made a mental note of the name as Lara continued in a low, fierce tone.

"The walls are thin. The doors, too. I hear them arguing as I pass by. He calls her a whore."

"That fits. Dammit, that fits."

Lara sat back, blinking in surprise.

"Barlow has a taste for high-priced call girls," Dodge explained.

They were both silent for a moment, each weighing the significance of what they'd learned.

"So he is there," Lara said slowly. "So he knows Elena. It is not a crime in Russia to use the services of what you term a 'call girl.'"

"Maybe not, but it does make him vulnerable to blackmail. Especially if this Elena Dimitri was feeding information on a member of the U.S. International Trade Delegation to the FSB."

"If she was, Bugarin will discover it," Lara returned with fierce satisfaction. "I told him her name earlier."

"Good. And while he's working his sources, I'll work mine. 'Scuse me."

Frowning, she watched him flip up his cell phone. He pressed a single number and waited the second or two for the system to verify his biometrics.

"Yo," Blade answered. "Something else happening out there?"

"Plenty. Right now, though, I need you to confirm Hank Barlow was in Moscow on the sixteenth of October six years ago."

"Hang on." A few clicks of a keyboard later, he was back. "Confirmed."

Dodge met Lara's intense gaze and nodded. She let loose with what he guessed was a vicious curse in Russian while he laid another task on Blade.

"Now find out everything you can about his relationship to a Russian woman, name of Elena Dimitri."

"That might take a little longer."

"Understood. Get back to me when you can."

He hung up to find Lara had pushed out of her chair and was regarding him with a frown.

"Who do you speak to that responds to you so

quickly? Air Force Special Investigations? The Defense Intelligence Agency? The CIA?"

The chasm opened again. Dodge couldn't leap it completely this time.

"Let's just say my contact has sources in all three of those agencies."

"So…? So you are a spy?" she gasped. "Dear God above, what have I done?"

He crossed the room in two strides. "You can trust me, Lara. I won't betray you or your mission. I swear it."

"How can I believe that?"

"You wouldn't be here if you didn't."

He underscored that point in the only way he could. By framing her face with his hands and lowering his head to brush his mouth over hers.

"And I," he murmured against her lips, "wouldn't be so damn crazy with wanting you."

She stood rigid beneath his kiss for so long Dodge thought he'd lost her. Then, just as he was about to admit defeat, her mouth opened under his.

The effect was electric. In an instant, he went from hungry to hard and aching. He brought her closer, felt her lean, supple length press against him. The intimate contact made her as wild as it did him. Her arms locked around his neck. Her tongue found his.

He found the clip that held her hair and worked it loose. The thick, silky mass tumbled free. Groaning, he threaded his fingers through it and drank in the taste of her. Countries, ideologies, cultural differences all melted away, until there was just him and her… and Dodge's driving need to discover how many layers she had on beneath her navy pantsuit.

Only two, he discovered to his instant delight. The black turtleneck and prim, white cotton underwear. The first layer he eliminated standing up. The second layer he reserved until he'd swept her into his arms, carried her to the bedroom and shed his own layers.

She didn't say a word when he joined her on the wide mattress. Nor did she try to hide the puckered flesh that stretched from the underside of her jaw to her shoulder. But the soft kiss he dropped on the side of her neck started a shudder that began at her shoulders and shimmied down her entire body.

"Does it hurt when I touch you there?"

"No. But…"

"But what?"

Despite the pride that kept her from covering her scars, Lara couldn't suppress a wave of shame. Her disfigurement had made her the object of so many embarrassed or pitying glances over the years.

"They are not beautiful, these scars."

"No, they're not."

She stiffened at his ready agreement. The heat lessened in her belly, only to flare hot and bright again when he brushed another kiss along her jaw.

"But you are, Larissa Petrovna. So beautiful you make me hurt."

His voice was so soft, his touch so caressing, she bit back the denial that rose to her lips. Then he planed his palm down her stomach and she bit back a gasp, as well. His tongue and teeth worked erotic magic on her neck, her breasts, her belly.

"You're like a winter night." His breath washed hot on her skin. "Moonlight on snow. Gold on silver. You take my breath away."

He exaggerated. Greatly. She was too pale, too thin. Her hip bones protruded. Her ribs showed like an old washboard. But her breasts were full and heavy when he freed them from the cotton. And when he suckled like a babe and drew her nipples into tight, aching points, murmuring outrageous gallantries all the while, she almost believed him.

He was so skilled, this cowboy. So incredibly skilled. He knew just where to stroke, where to press. He talked to her all the while he played with her, kissing, nipping, soothing where he stung.

And his hands! She could not believe his hands! Sandpapery rough, his fingers moved over her, slipped between her thighs, slid into her. Within moments, he had Lara arching her back. Mere seconds more, she screamed.

"You feel like silk." His fingers moved with maddening deliberation. His tongue and teeth tormented her ear. "Hot, wet…"

"No more words!" she hissed, jerking her head away. "I need no more words."

His grin popped out, so wicked that her breath stuck in her throat. "Fine by me. I'll save them for next time."

Rolling to the side of the bed, he scooped his pants from the floor and fished his wallet from his pocket. A moment later, he snapped on a condom with an expertise that left Lara in no doubt he'd done it many, many times before.

Torn between exasperation at his handy supply of contraceptives and relief that he carried one, she could only sigh when he turned back to her. There was nothing of the too-cocky American cowboy in him now.

Only elemental male, primed and ready. He was broad of shoulder. Ridged with muscle. His sack rode tight between his legs. His sex jutted thick, glistening within its plastic sheath.

In one swift move, he covered her and pressed her deep into the mattress. She spread her thighs, gave him entry. With a flex of his buttocks, he pushed in, pulled out, pushed in again. Bending her legs, Lara locked them around his thighs and made the movements her own.

She knew a fleeting stab of sorrow for the husband she'd lost and would never again hold in her arms. She also knew she would pay for this insanity. Bugarin would be waiting for her when she returned to her room, so furious at her prolonged absence that his fleshy jowls would quiver like suet. He'd demand a full report, know if she lied.

At this moment, she didn't care. For an hour or two or three, she would not let herself think about what had come before or would come after. Right now, for this small atom of time, she would not think at all.

Then Dodge rose on his elbows and tangled his fists in her hair to drag her head back. His eyes gleamed down at her. So intent. So intense.

He flexed his hips, surging into her with such raw power that he pushed her up against the backboard. Gasping, Lara dug her fingers into his shoulders. They bunched under her hands, slick, smooth.

Her release came so fast she barely had time to prepare for it. Like a missile igniting, the first stage engulfed her in a fury of heat that arched her back and ripped a groan from deep in her throat. Two heartbeats later, she shot straight into orbit. Dodge followed with a muffled grunt.

After the first time, he held her cradled against his side. She rested her head on his shoulder and told him of her parents, of her decision to make a career of the military, of Katya. He spoke of his youth, of the absurdity Americans called the rodeo, of his love of flying.

After the second time, they slept.

Only when the night pressed in on them and they rose to dress did they confront the matter that had brought them to this place.

"How long do you think it will be until you hear something from this contact of yours?" Lara asked as she tugged her sweater over her wildly tangled hair.

"Tomorrow. Next day at the latest. How about Bugarin?"

Her nose wrinkled. "He must go through eight levels of bureaucracy. But with the urgency of our mission, it will be fast."

"Good." The feral glint of a hunter came into his eyes. "I want all my ducks in a row when I pay our friend Barlow a visit."

"He is no friend of mine," Lara said fiercely. "But

know this, Dodge Hamilton. When you go, I go with you."

When he looked as though he would protest, she flung up a hand.

"I am determined on this. Do not even *try* to deny me."

"No, ma'am."

She weighed the response with suspicion. Did he mock her? Would he slip away after he received the information he sought?

She would watch him, Lara decided. During the day tomorrow, while they conducted the next scheduled missile inspection. During the night, as well. The thought sent a shaft of sensual anticipation straight to her belly.

Shaken by the sensation this man roused in her, Lara threw on her coat and stalked toward the door.

"Wait."

He grabbed his jacket, moving her to protest.

"You don't need to accompany me."

"Yeah, I do."

No way Dodge was letting her walk across the deserted parking lot this late, alone. Whoever planted that bug on her window could be watching, waiting. The possibility hunched his shoulders and kept him on full alert as they exited his building.

The rain had ended at last. The clouds had moved on and a million stars studded the dark sky. Dodge drew in a breath of the sharp, clean air, then pushed it out again when a figure in camouflage BDUs stepped out of the shadows. He carried a Heckler & Koch automatic nested in the crook of one arm. The subdued patch of the 90th Security Forces Group was barely visible on his cap.

"Looks like Colonel Yarboro's not going to allow any other unauthorized individual access to your team," he murmured approvingly.

The sentry pointed his weapon's muzzle groundward and approached. Dodge recognized him as one of the military police who'd guarded the convoy on several inspections.

He recognized them as well, and tipped two fingers to his hat brim. "Evenin', Major Petrovna."

"Good evening."

His glance flicked to Dodge. "'Evenin', sir. Out kind of late, aren't you?"

"So we are."

"Yeah, well, *impavide*."

"Thanks."

When he melted into the shadows, Lara frowned. "What is this impavide?"

"The motto of the 90th Missile Wing. It translates

to 'undaunted' in polite company. Something different after a few beers. C'mon, let's get you inside."

After the sharp night air, the heat of the hallway sucked the breath from their lungs. Their footfalls echoed in the empty corridor. Dodge waited until Lara had unlocked her door and he'd checked the interior of her apartment before sliding his arm around her waist.

"About tonight?"

"Yes?"

"I don't know where this thing between us is going, but…"

"It can go nowhere."

"But wherever it goes," he continued with a rueful grin, "it's going to be one hell of a ride."

She didn't answer for long moments. Then she muttered something that sounded very much like the Russian equivalent of "what the hell," and dragged his head down to hers.

Chapter 9

Dodge checked in with Blade at oh-six-hundred the next morning to confirm OMEGA's electronics wizards were hard at work dissecting the bug.

"No detailed info as yet," Blade related. "Mac says the coating on the transmission fiber is some kind of new composite she hasn't seen before. She has her folks researching recent patent applications to see who manufactured it."

"If it tracks to E-Systems," Dodge vowed grimly, "I'm hitting the road for Denver."

"I hear you."

"How about Elena Dimitri? Anything on her yet?"

"Our contact in Moscow is still working on that. I'll let you know as soon as I hear something."

"Thanks. By the way, you might want to advise Lightning that I crossed a line with Major Petrovna last night. One I can't…correction, one I don't *want* to back away from."

Blade gave a long, low whistle but didn't ask for details. They both knew the risks and penalties that particular line-crossing could entail.

"I'll tell him."

With that laconic promise, Dodge disconnected and got ready for the day's inspection. His air-force flight suit fit like an old friend. So did the sidearm he decided to strap on.

His weapon of choice on other OMEGA ops was a Smith & Wesson .45 with a laser sight and enough wallop to bring down a charging moose. Since he was at F. E. Warren in the alter ego of a USAF chopper pilot, he'd opted for the standard military-issue .9-mm Beretta for this mission.

With a snap of the slide, Dodge checked the chamber to make sure it was empty before tucking the Beretta into its holster. The spare magazine clip he slipped into the leg pocket of his flight suit. The weapon's weight rested reassuringly against his hip as he exited the VOQ.

The predawn air was sharp and clean but the

temperature had dropped a good forty degrees overnight. Dodge's breath clouded as he crossed the parking lot. Security forces were still guarding Lara's building. A sentry Dodge didn't recognize stopped him, eyed his holstered Beretta and asked to see some ID. He matched Dodge's face to the photo on his military ID and consulted an access list.

"You're cleared in, sir."

Nodding, Dodge took back his ID and returned the guard's salute. A slightly breathless Lara answered his knock a few moments later.

"Come in. I have only to put up my hair and I am ready."

She displayed no morning-after awkwardness, no shyness or hesitancy. Yet the hours they'd spent tangled in the sheets showed in the slightly bemused smile she gave him. As if she couldn't quite believe he'd gotten past her prickly defenses. Or that she'd let him.

While she twisted the white-gold mass of her hair and anchored it with a plastic clip, Dodge's gaze roamed her slender figure. The memory of how perfectly she'd fit against him put a husky edge to his voice.

"You'd better take your cold-weather gear."

She snatched up the field jacket and headed across

the room. The sight of his holster stopped her in midstride. Frowning, she lifted her gaze to his.

"It is necessary, this weapon?"

"Just a precaution."

"They will let you take it into a missile site?"

She clucked her tongue, as if to say such a thing would never happen in Russia, and started toward him again. Dodge's bulk blocked her way.

"Did you tell Bugarin about last night?"

"It was too late when I returned. I will tell him today, after the inspection."

"It's going to cost you," Dodge said quietly. "You could be putting your career on the line."

"I know this." She cocked her head. "And you? Have you reported our...our transgression to your superiors?"

"I have."

"What did they say?"

"It was pretty much a one-sided conversation," he admitted with a grin. "I expect I'll get more feedback later."

"Your career, too, may suffer."

"I'm not worried about it." His grin softened. "You're worth whatever comes, Larissa."

He took her breath away. The smile in his eyes. The caress in his voice. His gentleness unnerved Lara almost as much as the hunger that rose in her for his touch.

"We…we must go," she said gruffly.

They followed the scripted routine. Breakfast with the other team members and their escorts. Rendezvous at the staging area. Convoy out to the site.

This time the designated launch facility was Charlie-3, located just the other side of Scotts Bluff, Nebraska, more than two hours away from the base. And this time, two choppers flew convoy support instead of the usual one. Each bird carried a full compliment of heavily armed security forces. Although there was nothing to link the listening device Bugarin had discovered to possible terrorist activity, the 90th Missile Wing commander wasn't taking any chances.

Every time a shadow swooped over the bus, Dodge's palms itched. He would much rather be up there at the controls with an eagle's view of the surrounding terrain and any potential threats, instead of bouncing along inside an overheated bus. Particularly since the vehicle rolled through mile after mile of undulating plains broken only by the occasional rock formation that jutted out of the ground like a silent sentinel.

The two-hour trip seemed to take forever. Even his chopper pilot's bladder was feeling the strain by the time the convoy halted for the chief of the security team to coordinate with their arrival at the site with the Missile Alert Facility. After an extended security check, the MAF cleared them into the fenced site. As on previous inspections, the drivers swung their vehicles around and parked them pointing toward the gate for quick egress if necessary.

The Beretta's weight slapped reassuringly against Dodge's hip as the Russians and their escorts all made a quick trip to the camper's latrine facilities. Returning to the bus, they waited while the maintenance and security forces positioned the payload transporter over the silo and went through the prolonged procedures for accessing the missile itself.

While the maintainers worked, a real screamer howled down from the north. The vicious wind flattened the prairie grasses and reddened the faces of the personnel working topside. The inspection team climbed out of the bus to verify the coordinates of the site, then climbed right back in.

Dodge felt restless and more than a little useless sitting in the stuffy warmth of the bus. Those feelings piled up like the clouds building on the horizon. Finally, the Minuteman III nestled inside the payload transporter. With the wind beating them, the inspection team crossed the enclosure and climbed into the PT. Bugarin entered and left the frigid, boxcar structure quickly, as did Captain Tsychenko. Lara stayed inside almost the entire time. Hands tucked under her arms for warmth, she stood only inches from the missile and watched the crew do their scheduled maintenance with the intensity of a hawk.

When the convoy prepared for the return trip to Warren some hours later, the Missile Alert Facility notified them of a weather alert. State police had closed the primary route due to icing on the overpasses. They needed at least another hour to verify that the bridges and overpasses on the alternate route had been salted and sanded. The convoy couldn't leave the site. The crews who'd finished their work could, however, make a dash into Scotts Bluff for a badly needed hot meal. All nonessential personnel piled onto the bus for the short drive.

The red rock formation that gave the city its name rose some eight hundred feet above the North Platte River. A familiar landmark to emigrants traveling the Oregon, California and Mormon trails, the towering promontory cut like a ship's prow through the angry sky.

By mutual consent, the occupants of the bus

voted to bypass the downtown area and stop at the airport restaurant for hot coffee, a solid meal and, most important, one of the eatery's homemade sticky buns. Fat, fried and dripping with gooey icing, the doughy confections were a favorite with missile and aircrews alike.

"You have to try one," Dodge told Lara once they were inside.

"I am so hungry, perhaps I shall eat two. But first I must find the restroom."

She wove a zigzag path through tables crowded with personnel wearing airport employee IDs. Scattered among them were passengers waiting out the weather delay and several hunters in orange caps and camouflage overalls.

The women's restroom was small and tucked away at the end of a long hall. Once inside, Lara grimaced at the tumbled strands that had blown free of their plastic clip and now hung over her jacket collar. She fought the clip free and dragged a comb through the tangles. Wincing, she tugged at the wind-whipped snarls. She had considered hacking off the heavy mass often over the years, but Yuri...

Her comb stilled.

Yuri had loved it long. He would comb his fingers through it when they were alone, sometimes absently, sometimes as a prelude to love play.

The memory stirred a touch of panic in Lara's chest. Why could she not see her husband's face? Why could she not recall the exact hue of his eyes? Six years had passed, only six years.

She knew the reason, had raged against the unfairness of it many times. The simple fact was that she had nothing to remind her of Yuri's face, no memento to remember him by. The fire had destroyed everything. Their clothes. Their furnishings. Even their past.

No photographs had been found in the ashes, not the studio portrait of both of them in uniform the day they married, nor the snapshots at the Black Sea resort where they vacationed the summer before she became pregnant. Nothing had survived of their life together.

Nothing except Katya, and there was so little of Yuri in her. Every month, every year, Lara had to search harder for the father's traits in the daughter. And now...

Now she had to search even harder for memories of her husband. She'd let her career consume her. And this mission. And a certain American cowboy who'd suddenly, unexpectedly, crowded his way into her life.

Shaking her head, Lara jammed the comb into her jacket pocket and yanked on the door handle.

She strode out, only to crash into a man making his way down the hall to the restroom. Stumbling back, she would have tripped over her own feet if he hadn't caught her by her sleeve.

"Forgive me," she said, annoyed by her own clumsiness.

He frowned at her from under the brim of his red ball cap, his eyes shadowed and oddly intent. Belatedly, she realized she'd spoken in Russian.

"I am sorry," she repeated in English.

He tipped the brim of his cap to her and stepped aside.

"I waited to go through the line with you," Dodge told her when she reached the table.

Digging the black change purse that held her meager supply of dollars out of her pocket, Lara unzipped the heavy jacket and tossed it over the back of her chair.

"Let us go."

The meal passed in silence. Still shaken by the realization that Dodge Hamilton's face had supplanted that of her husband's in her mind, Lara crumbled a bread roll into her bowl of vegetable soup but could spoon down only half the hearty portion. She finished long before Aleksei Bugarin, who stuffed salad, chopped sirloin steak, mashed potatoes, corn, white bread and three sweet buns into his bulging jowls. When Lara refused one of the sticky confections, Dodge threw her a quick glance.

"You sure? This is a fresh batch, just out of the oven. Why don't you try one? My treat."

"If I wished one, I would purchase it."

The sharp response hiked his brows and brought Bugarin's head up. His glance went from her to Dodge and back again. The sudden suspicion in his dark eyes made Lara bite the inside of her cheek. She didn't look forward to confessing the truth to him when they were alone.

"If you have finished…?" she asked with frigid politeness.

"Yes, yes."

He crammed in the last bite and grabbed his jacket from the back of his chair. Lara, Captain Tyschenko and their escorts did the same.

Dusk had fallen during their brief respite and the cold cut like a sword. Lara huddled in her seat on the bus, hands tucked into her armpits for warmth, until the vehicle's heater chased the chill from the air and her jacket raised a sweat. Shrugging out of the heavy garment once again, she stared through the window at the gathering darkness.

The icy roads made the return trip to Cheyenne an agonizing crawl. By the time the convoy pulled into the staging area a little past 9:00 p.m., she ached with weariness and the strain of nerves stretched thin. Her limbs heavy, she gathered her gear and transferred to Dodge's vehicle for the ride back to her quarters.

"I need to make some calls," he told her as he pulled up at the door to her building. "I'll come over as soon as I'm done."

"No." Wearily, she scrubbed the heel of her hand across her brow. "I must speak to Bugarin. It will not be a pleasant encounter."

He searched her face and saw the weariness she didn't even try to disguise.

"Okay, we'll do this your way. Tonight."

He waited with the engine running while the guard on duty screened Lara and permitted her to pass. At the entrance to the building she slipped a hand in her jacket pocket.

Instead of her room key, her fingers encountered what felt like paper. Surprised, she withdrew a folded sheet. She didn't remember stuffing anything in the pocket except her comb, her change purse and her key. Frowning, she unfolded the sheet and tipped it toward the light.

Her heart contracted, swift and hard. The lights beside the entrance dimmed and went black for a moment. When her vision cleared, Lara stared with her heart slamming against her sternum at the faxed photo of her daughter.

The pigtailed Katya walking into the schoolyard with her best friend, Leoninya. They had their satchels slung over their shoulders. Identical grins spread across their scrubbed faces.

The photo cut into Lara like a knife to the heart, but it was the scrawled message at the bottom of the page that started the blood roaring in her ears.

A taxi will pick you up at midnight. Say nothing—to anyone—or your daughter dies.

"Major?"

The guard's voice barely penetrated the terror hazing Lara's mind.

"Major Petrovna?"

A car door slammed. Footsteps rang on the sidewalk. Dodge called to her.

"Lara? Something wrong?"

Say nothing to anyone or your daughter dies.

Crumpling the fax into a tight wad, Lara buried her fist in her pocket.

"*Nyet.* I…I but look for my key. It is here, in my pocket."

She would never know how she forced the words. She was frozen, inside and out. A thick coat of ice encased her every organ. She couldn't think, couldn't breathe, couldn't see anything except the image of Katya, pinned in the crosshairs of a camera lens.

"You all right?" Dodge asked on a note of sharp concern.

Say nothing to anyone.

"I am merely tired."

"You look more than just tired. You look like you've seen a ghost."

Ghosts. They surrounded her. Yuri. Elena Dimitri. Her friends and neighbors who'd died in the fire. The man whose voice she'd heard that awful night six years ago. She wanted to scream at them, to beg them all to leave her in peace. To leave her daughter in peace!

Instead, she pushed through the outer entrance and walked blindly down the hall. Dodge followed, still concerned. Outside her door, she forced herself to release the crumpled fax and retrieve her key from her pocket.

She managed to insert it into the lock after only one fumbling attempt. Stepping inside on legs that felt as though they would collapse at any instant, she flipped the light switch and turned.

"Good night, Dodge."

Stepping back, she shut the door again. The moment the lock clicked into place, Lara threw the key aside and reached frantically for the wadded paper.

Katya. Her baby.

Hands shaking, she smoothed the wrinkles. Her daughter's bright smile stabbed into her chest. Katya wore her school uniform. Carried her satchel of books. And…

Those earphones draped around her neck! They went with the iPod Lara had purchased and mailed just after she'd arrived. Katya could only have received it a day or two ago. Which meant the photo had to have been taken yesterday…or today!

Frantic, Lara raced for the phone on the desk. Her fingers stabbed the international number she used so sparingly during her travels.

Finally—*finally!*—the school administrator answered. Lara all but shouted into the phone.

"This is Larissa Petrovna."

"Hello, Major. Are you back from your trip? I thought you were not to return until…"

"My daughter! I must know! She is there?"

"Katya? Yes, she's here. I saw her in the hallway just a half hour ago."

"Get her! Please, I must speak with her."

She waited the longest minutes of her life with the phone jammed to her ear and long-forgotten prayers tumbling from her lips.

"Mama?"

She couldn't push a single word through the thick relief that clogged her throat.

"Mama? Is that you? Are you calling from America?"

Forcing down panic, joy, terror, Lara clutched the phone. "Yes, baby. I just wanted to make sure you're all right."

"Oh, Mama! Thank you for the iPod! It came yesterday." The girl's bubbly enthusiasm spilled across the miles. "All my friends want to listen to…"

She broke off, wheezing the way she always did when she got too excited.

"Slowly, Katya. You must speak slowly."

The admonition came automatically, without thinking. From the mother, not the woman so filled with fear for her child she couldn't draw in a whole breath herself.

"Listen to me, baby. Call Natalia. Have her come to the school to pick you up. Tell her to take you…"

Where? Where would her child be safe?

Not in the Moscow apartment, Lara realized with choking helplessness. Nor at her babysitter's. Whoever had arranged for that photo to be taken knew where she went to school, where she lived.

Say nothing to anyone or your daughter dies.

"Katya, listen to me. I'm going to call Colonel Zacharov. You remember him, don't you?"

"He's your boss, Mama. I remember him."

Zacharov was more than her boss. He was her mentor, her friend. He'd once been Yuri's commander. He now directed Russia's military-intelligence community. Lara trusted him as she could trust no one else. If anyone could keep Katya safe it was Zacharov.

"He'll come for you, Katya. Go with him, all right? And…and…" Her throat burned. "Be good, baby."

She got through to Zacharov's office a few minutes later. He wasn't there, forcing Lara to relay her urgent request to his aide. He promised to contact his superior immediately.

"Call me," she begged. "Please. As soon as you speak to the colonel."

When he agreed, she dropped the phone onto its cradle. Her hands shook as she smoothed the crumpled fax and stared down at it with burning eyes.

Who had slipped it into her pocket? When?

She tried to think back, tried to remember the times the green Gortex jacket had been out of her immediate possession. Last week, when she left it in Dodge's rented SUV after the accident. Last night, when she'd spent those stolen hours with Dodge.

And today, she remembered in a blinding flash. At the restaurant. When she draped the garment over the back of her chair and joined the long line at the grill. Anyone could have brushed past her chair, slipped something into her pocket.

Or collided with her in the narrow hallway outside the restrooms.

Her stomach lurched. Had he been waiting for her, the stranger in the red ball cap? Had he anticipated her emergence from the bathroom? Put himself directly in her path?

Desperately, Lara tried to remember his face, his features. All she could recall was his intent look and the way he'd dipped the brim of his hat in acknowledgment of her muttered apologies.

Had he remained silent so she would not recognize his voice? The possibility hit with the force of a blow. In her heart she knew—she *knew*—that he was either Henry Barlow or one of his hirelings. Perhaps the same hireling had driven the black SUV that had forced Dodge's Jeep off the road.

Her first instinct was to run across the parking lot and hammer on Dodge's door. Her second, to obey the ominous instructions.

Say nothing to anyone or your daughter dies.

A wave of hate swept through her, so raw and hot it thawed the ice around her heart. Someone would most certainly die, she vowed with all the ferocity of her Cossack ancestors. Someone would die before the next sun rose.

Striding into the kitchen, she yanked open the drawer containing the cooking utensils. Her jaw clamped tight, she pulled out a small cutting knife and tested its blade against her thumb. A thin red ribbon welled up where the serrated blade sliced into her skin.

Welcoming the pain and the warm trickle of blood, Lara sat down and waited for the clock to tick away the minutes until midnight.

Chapter 10

Blade had a grainy black-and-white surveillance video up on the screen of the console when Mackenzie Blair Jensen sailed into the control center. Although it was close to 4:00 a.m., the mother of lively twin boys looked as fresh and bright-eyed as she had when she'd assembled her team almost twenty-four hours ago.

The woman who entered with her looked even better. Her combination of honey-blond hair, mile-long legs and black leather could jump-start a dead man's pulse.

His visceral reaction to Victoria Talbot had Blade delivering a swift mental kick in the butt. Rebel had let him know in no uncertain terms that it was—and would remain—strictly business between them.

"We got him," Mac announced gleefully.

"Barlow?"

"Right." Grinning, she hooked a strand of mink-brown hair behind her ear. "The coating on the fiber in the bug threw me for a while. I've never seen that mix of polymers used on a communications device before."

"Because it's never *been* used in a communications device before?" Blade guessed.

"Right again." Her brown eyes gleamed with the thrill of a successful hunt. "We spent hours researching patents and Federal Communications Commission new-product applications. Rebel was the one who suggested we tap into NASA's database. And there it was, buried in a bid to upgrade the space shuttle's cockpit voice-retrieval system."

Rebel shrugged as if to downplay her role in the discovery, but the excitement was there. Blade felt the vibes as Mac continued.

"The bid described a new composite that can supposedly withstand everything from the intense cold of deep space to the heat of reentry. So new that it's still in final research and development at E-Systems."

"Bingo," Blade said softly.

"It's a link," Rebel concurred. "But a loose one.

There could be upward of a hundred people at E-Systems working R&D of new products."

Blade's glance cut to the computer screen on the command console. "But only one who was tagged in a CIA surveillance video leaving a Moscow nightclub with Elena Dimitri less than an hour before her death."

Neither Mac nor Rebel questioned how OMEGA's Moscow contact had gained access to a CIA surveillance tape. But they hovered at Blade's shoulder to watch it.

He ran it once, then again. The video was only about forty seconds long but it established the fact that Hank Barlow was one of the last people to see Elena Dimitri alive.

"I'd better pass this info to Dodge and Lightning," Blade said when the tape flickered out.

"You contact Dodge and I'll call my husband," Mac said. "I need to let him know I'm on my way home to relieve him of daddy duty."

"In the meantime," Rebel added, nudging Blade aside to get at the console. "I'll verify Barlow boy's whereabouts. I have a feeling Dodge is gonna want to get up close and personal with him. If not tonight, then first thing in the morning."

Blade stifled a surge of annoyance. Damned if the woman hadn't butted in on his op again. He'd have to break her of that habit, and soon. Reaching around her, he keyed in a number.

Dodge had just drifted into sleep when his phone buzzed. He came awake instantly, checked the code on the digital display and had the phone to his ear by the second buzz.

"What've you got for me?"

He knew it had to be good. Blade wouldn't call this late without reason.

It was better than good. His gut tightened when Blade relayed that E-Systems was the only known manufacturer of what was still considered an experimental hyperconductive polymer. The CIA surveillance video tightened it another notch.

"Time for me to head down to Denver," he told Blade grimly.

"That's what we figured you would say. Rebel's on the other line now, verifying Barlow's whereabouts."

A moment later she made it a three-way conversation.

"Surveillance shows he departed his residence at nineteen-ten this evening with an as-yet unidentified male. They took the other guy's vehicle."

Hell! So much for tagging Barlow's personal and company cars with GPS.

"Did they go out to E-Systems?"

"Negative."

The reply set off every one of Dodge's internal alarms. "Hang loose! I want to check on Lara."

He dialed the number for her VOQ room. His chest squeezed harder with each unanswered ring. Swearing, he switched back to Blade and Rebel.

"She doesn't answer. I'm going over there."

The flight suit he'd tossed over the back of a chair was the closest item at hand. It took Dodge two minutes flat to zip himself into it and stomp his feet into his boots. Shoving his phone into a pocket, he snatched up the Beretta.

He crossed the parking lot at a dead run that brought the security guards out of the shadows, assault rifles at the ready. One of them made a visual ID. The other responded to Dodge's sharp query.

"Anyone who doesn't have access to this building try to get in?"

"Not on our watch, sir." He eyed Dodge closely in the dim light. "Is there a problem?"

"Major Petrovna's not answering her phone."

"That's because she's not here. She departed the VOQ about a half hour ago in a commercial taxi."

"A taxi?"

"Yes, sir. Cheyenne Cab Company."

Thrown for a loop, Dodge tried to make sense of that. "Was she alone?"

"Yes, sir."

"Under duress?"

"Not that I could see."

"Did you ask where she was going?"

"No, sir."

Dodge didn't like this. Where would Lara go by herself at this time of night? His gaze swept the building, noting the light that spilled from two sets of windows. One set belonged to Lara. The other he was certain belonged to Bugarin.

The FSB officer wasn't in his room, either. Dodge spotted him inserting a key into Lara's door. In the glow of the wall-mounted lights, his complexion showed pasty white.

"You make a habit of letting yourself into other people's rooms?" Dodge bit out.

"I have the key. I am authorized."

"Like hell you are."

"I have received a communiqué," the FSB officer blustered. "I must speak with Major Petrovna. She does not answer my knock, so I use my key."

"She's not there."

The FSB officer gaped, his black eyes almost popping from their nest of puffy flesh. "Where is she?"

"I don't know."

"How can you not know? You are her escort!"

He didn't bother responding to that and focused instead on Bugarin's revelation. "You indicated you received a communiqué. What did it say?"

The Russian hesitated, caught between Lara's unexplained absence and his ingrained suspicion of any and all Americans. Both emotions seemed to boil over an instant later.

"I am being recalled." Bitterness gushed from the man in almost palpable spurts. "Immediately. I am to pack my bags and leave on the first flight this very morning."

"Why?"

He flung a hand toward Lara's door. "Because of this stupid bitch."

When Dodge made a sound deep in his throat, Bugarin's mouth twisted into a sneer.

"She has played her games with you, hasn't she? She's a whore, that one. Just like…"

He broke off, gasping as Dodge grabbed his shirtfront and slammed him against the wall.

"You're two seconds away from dead, you little turd."

"You cannot…! The treaty!"

"The hell with the treaty. Tell me about this communiqué. Did it include any information about Hank Barlow?"

"No, no!" The FSB officer clawed at the choke hold. "It said only that I am to cease all inquiries regarding a woman by the name of Elena Dimitri and return to Moscow immediately."

His mind racing, Dodge let the man drop. He could think of only one reason for the FSB to come down so hard. Barlow had friends in high places.

Scooping up the key Bugarin had dropped during the scuffle, Dodge shoved it into the lock on Lara's door. A quick check of her rooms confirmed the sentry's report. She was gone. So was the jacket he'd obtained for her from central supply.

Jaw set, Dodge whipped out his phone. Luckily, there was only one cab company in town.

"This is Major Hamilton, F. E. Warren," he rasped at the sleepy dispatcher who answered. "One of your drivers picked up a customer at the Visiting Officers' Quarters here on base about a half hour ago. I need to know where he took her."

"We're not s'posed to give out that kind of information but, well, this one's kinda strange."

"Strange how?"

"The driver radioed in just a few minutes ago. Said he dropped his passenger off at a rest stop on I-40, forty-two miles west of Cheyenne."

"Forty-two miles west." Dodge painted a map inside his head. "That's almost to Laramie. Hell, I know that stop. There's nothing there but a cement slab with restrooms and a couple of trash cans."

"Like I said, it's kinda strange."

It was a whole lot more than strange, but Dodge didn't have time for explanations. He slapped the phone shut and was about to spin for the door when he saw Bugarin stoop to retrieve a crumpled piece of paper from under the desk. The FSB officer straightened, smoothed the paper and went pasty white. Wordlessly, he held it out.

Dodge recognized the smiling pigtailed girl instantly. The scrawled warning below the picture brought the breath hissing out of his lungs.

He spun toward the door again and hit the hall on a dead run. Crashing out into the parking lot, he shouted at the guard who leaped from the shadows.

"Call Colonel Yarboro. Tell him Major Petrovna is missing and get his authorization for me to take up the alert bird. I'm on my way to the 37th now."

The 37th Helicopter Squadron kept a chopper fueled and ready at all times. They had to, to support the wing's twenty-four-hour missile-alert requirements. The Huey could also be used when requested by civilian authorities for MAST—Military Assistance to Safety and Traffic. Dodge could care less how the squadron classified this mission as long as they got the bird in the air ASAP.

Tires squealing, he peeled out of the parking lot. As he tore across base, he used one hand to steer and the other to get his OMEGA controller on the net. Blade sucked air when Dodge bit out the latest developments.

"Contact the Wyoming Highway Patrol. Have them get a patrol car out to the rest stop, like, now!"

"Will do."

When Dodge screeched to a halt on the ramp behind the 37th's flight-ops building, the sound of engines revving filled his ears. Colonel Yarboro hadn't wasted any time.

Nor had the maintenance personnel. Most of them were former air force who'd opted out of the military and into the civilian corporation that provided support for a number of military chopper units in the Western U.S. Combined, they represented probably over three hundred years of experience on the Huey.

As a consequence, the craft was straining at the chocks when Dodge ducked under the whirring blades and yanked open the cockpit door. The familiar face of the helo squadron commander greeted him across the controls. Surprised, Dodge slapped on a headset and keyed the mike.

"You pulling alert tonight, Digger?"

"The captain who had duty came down with the flu. Figured I'd stand in for him and log some alert hours. What's the big emergency?"

"Major Petrovna from the Russian inspection team has gone missing."

The colonel formed a soundless whistle. "That's gonna play hell with the START treaty."

Dodge didn't give a rat's ass about the treaty right now. Fear for Lara sat like a hard, cold rock in his stomach.

"Her last known location was a rest stop forty-two miles due west on I-40. I need you to get me there, ASAP."

"We'll be airborne in five minutes," McGee promised.

He punched the location into the mission-planning computer and strapped on a pair of night-vision goggles. After running through the last preflight checklist with the engineer, he revved the engine and lifted off.

Dodge spotted their destination while they were still some miles away. A highway patrol car flashing red and blue strobes had already arrived on the scene. Its headlights stabbed through the darkness of the Wyoming night and highlighted the two eighteen-wheelers parked along the ramp leading into the rest area.

After scanning the access road and finding a spot well clear of both the rigs and the wooden snow fence designed to keep winter drifts from blowing across the interstate, Digger keyed his mike.

"Rotor One, this is Rotor Eleven."

The duty officers' reply crackled through her headset. "Go ahead, Rotor Eleven."

"We're at our destination and touching down."

"Roger, Rotor eleven."

Bringing the Huey down was an exercise in skill and caution, made even more delicate by the blast of air every time another semi roared by on the interstate just yards away.

The skids had barely touched when Dodge jumped out. Digger stayed with the chopper while Dodge loped over to the uniformed officers. He knew they would have radioed in if they'd found Lara but had to ask anyway.

"Major Hamilton, from F. E. Warren. Any sign of the Russian woman we're searching for?"

"No, sir."

"What about those rigs? Did the drivers see anything?"

"One of the truckers says he saw a taxi drive up about ten, fifteen minutes ago. Thought it was odd, a taxi so far from town. Especially when the passenger got out and into another vehicle."

"Did he get the vehicle's make or tag number?"

"He was still half-asleep. Didn't think to note the license number, but says the vehicle was a dark-colored Ford Taurus."

Stolen the night before, Dodge guessed grimly, and wiped clean of all prints when it's found tomorrow. Barlow's hired guns were nothing if not careful. He climbed back in the cockpit a few minutes later and gave a terse report.

"She got into a dark-colored Taurus."

"Voluntarily?"

"Apparently. The Highway Patrol is putting up roadblocks east and west of here."

"They'll net him," Digger said with more assurance than Dodge could summon.

"Unless the bastard got off at the first Laramie exit and hit the side roads. He's slippery enough to plan for just this sort of contingency. How much fuel have we got?"

Digger read his mind. "More than enough to take this baby up and buzz one or two of those side roads."

It wasn't the most coherent plan of attack but it was better than sitting on his hands while Lara was out there somewhere, alone, with the bastard who'd threatened to kill her daughter.

Lara came awake slowly, painfully. A buzzing filled her ears. Pain blazed in her neck, her shoulder. She tried to raise her head, got it up a few inches, then it dropped forward, like a rag doll's.

"You surprise me, Larissa Petrovna."

The rasping whisper came to her through the wall of pain. Like a sword, it cut into her head and bludgeoned her whirling senses.

"Most men wouldn't recover from a jolt like that for a half hour or more."

Gritting her teeth against the agony, Lara forced her chin up, centimeter by whirling centimeter, until she could make out the man who stood before her, smiling.

Smiling!

Damn his soul!

"I know," he said with sympathy so false it raised a fury that burned away the last of her confusion. "These stun guns hurt, or so I've been told."

She remembered now. Getting out of the taxi. Shivering in the cold that knifed across the open highway. Huddling in the entrance to the ladies' room, her heart hammering, until the car drove up and someone reached across to open the passenger door.

It had swung in the wind, that open door. The interior was dark, so dark Lara could see nothing as she forced herself to walk to the car. She remembered sliding into the seat, turning her head toward the shadowy figure beside her and…

And pain. One lancing jolt in the side of her neck. She remembered nothing else.

Her blood felt as cold as the wind as she studied the one who watched her like a hawk. She didn't recognize him, couldn't remember ever seeing him before. He looked like any other man. Not short, not particularly tall. His face was handsome in a rugged sort of way, his leather jacket and designer jeans expensive.

"You…are…Barlow?"

"Yes. And you are the stubborn woman who wouldn't let sleeping ghosts lie."

"Wh…? Where…?"

She sounded just like him! A hoarse croak. A rusty wheeze. She slicked her tongue across her lips and tried again.

"Where have you brought me?"

Carefully, she turned her head. They were in a kitchen, she saw. An old kitchen, with windows of broken glass and walls with peeling strips of faded paper. There was a table, chairs. One had toppled on its side, missing a leg. She was taped into another. The light... She searched for the source. The light came from a powerful electric lantern set a few feet away. It kept her pinned in a vicious beam as Barlow replied to her question with a careless shrug.

"I believe the locals call this the old Miller place. I stumbled on it when I was up here hunting a few years ago."

Only now did Lara realize they spoke in Russian. His accent was pure Moscow, as fluid and idiomatic as hers. Was he Russian? One of the many moles sent to America over the years?

"Are you FSB?" she croaked.

Laughter broke from him, as rough and harsh as his voice. "A secret agent? Hardly. The job doesn't pay well enough."

A rustle from the shadows behind him told her they weren't alone, but Lara's entire being was focused on the one who mocked her with his smile.

"I have friends in the FSB, however. Well-placed friends who enjoy the rubles I pay them to look the other way on certain of my business dealings."

"Did you...?" Her breath hitched. Her heart pounded. After so many years, so many tears, she had to know. "Did you set the fire six years ago?"

"I did. Most regrettably, I assure you."

Her fingers curled into claws as she struggled against tape binding her wrists to the chair arms.

"Why?" she whispered.

"It was the only way I could think of at the time to dispose of the woman's body without implicating myself in her death."

"Elena." Hate boiled up in Lara's veins. "Her name was Elena. You killed her?"

"Not intentionally. Things just got a little out of hand that night. Even my friends in the FSB couldn't cover up something like that."

The reply was like a wire brush gouging her skin, drawing blood with each word.

"You bastard! You killed so many because of one?"

"I told you, things got out of hand. And the fire department took so long to respond. As they will tonight. This place is so far out in the country, you see."

Lara went still, absolutely still, as Barlow shot back his cuff and checked his watch.

"It won't happen for some hours yet, Larissa Petrovna. I have to drive back to my plant in Denver. The night shift will verify that I was miles away when this fire broke out and you so tragically perished."

He was so smug, so sure of himself. She would

have killed him with her bare hands at that moment had she been able to break free of the tape.

"They'll come and interrogate me, of course. They won't be able to tie me to anything, but they'll try. The OSI, who have already asked so many questions. The CIA. Your friend, Major Hamilton. How did you intend to explain the fact that you slept with him, I wonder?"

She answered with a curse that drew a shrug from her tormentor.

"Ah, well, you won't have to explain anything now, will you?"

He extracted something from his pocket. A tube of some sort. Lara guessed what it was even before he squeezed out a drop of gel that glistened in the bright light of the lantern.

"Such a useful tool, this new compound. It burns cleanly and leaves no trace."

He smoothed the gel onto the wall beside him, then reached into his pocket again for what looked like a spool of thread and a knife—the same small, serrated kitchen knife Lara had brought with her.

He didn't look her way as he cut a short length of thread. No, not thread. Wire. After inserting one end into the plastic, he attached the other to a cylinder of some sort. Then he extracted a cell phone and pressed its keys.

The small beeps thundered in silence. One. Two. A third. The wire puffed and spit sparks. Barlow blew them out and cut a longer length to replace the short one. When he was done, he tucked his implements in his pocket and turned to her for a last time.

"If you're lucky, Larissa Petrovna, the smoke will reach you before the flames."

"Katya…"

She hated to ask anything of this monster, loathed the plea in her voice, but she would cry, beg, sell her soul to the devil himself to save her baby.

"My daughter…"

"I won't have her harmed. Once you're dead, there's no need."

He left then, taking the light with him. Lara heard him say something to whomever waited for him. An engine turned over. Tires crunched on dirt. Then she was alone in the dark and the wind and the cold.

Chapter 11

The Huey responded like the tried-and-true work-horse it was. Swooping through the night sky, it skimmed across wide-open stretches while Dodge and the flight engineer scanned the roads below.

Night-vision goggles turned the darkness into green, shimmering light. The staticky hum of the radio buzzed in his ears as flight ops relayed updates from the highway patrol, county and local police units, and the Warren command post.

Dodge kept OMEGA in the loop, as well. Blade confirmed that neither Barlow's wife nor his personal assistant knew his present whereabouts.

"But he told his wife that he planned a late-night

visit to E-Systems' main production facility. Said he wants to talk to crew doing the tooling up for production of a new gyroscope."

"Covering his ass," Dodge snarled.

"Sounds like."

"How long is that particular crew on the line?"

"Plant manager says they go off shift at three a.m."

Dodge checked his watch. "It's almost two now. He can't be more than seventy, eighty miles out of Denver if he's going to hit the plant by three."

To make that kind of speed, he had to be traveling a main artery. That meant either I-25 or 287. The highway patrol was covering the interstate.

Playing the odds, Dodge keyed his mike. "Get us over 287, Digger, and lay on some speed."

Lara had fought against the constricting tape for what felt like hours, shivering convulsively, hating, fearing, weeping in frustration when she couldn't move her arms or legs. All she succeeded in doing was tipping the chair she was tied to onto its side and slamming into the dirt-strewn floor with a thud.

Dazed and panting, she lay with her cheek pressed to the grimy floorboards. She wasn't sure now why she'd struggled so hard to free herself. Pure instinct, she supposed.

But…

If she died here, her daughter would be safe. Katya knew nothing. She was no threat to Barlow or his friends at the FSB.

Lara almost gave up then. Almost let the memories of Katya as a baby, as a toddler, as a giggling little girl, comfort her last hours. If a gust of cold hadn't swept through a hole where the floorboards had rotted, she might have abandoned all further attempts to free herself.

Like a bucket of icy water, the blast of cold air revived both her determination and her will to live. She had no guarantee Barlow would stick to his word. And if she died here, Katya would have lost both father and mother to the same murderous bastard.

Jaw locked, Lara contorted as much as the constricting bonds would allow. If a nail protruded from just one of those rotten boards… If she could squirm sideways, like the crab…

Dodge peered through the night-vision goggles at the green glow spearing an empty stretch of 287. Traffic was light this time of night. So light, this was only the fifth or sixth set of headlights they'd swooped in on.

He leaned forward, straining to see, as Digger angled the collective. The Huey's blades changed pitch another few degrees. The nose tipped. The aircraft picked up speed.

Slowly, the distant spear resolved into two parallel beams. The night goggles amplified the heat put out by the engine to a hot green flash and gave shape to the vehicle itself.

"We got us a possible," Dodge said grimly.

"Hang on. I'm going in for a closer look."

Digger took them down to three hundred feet, two hundred, one. The Huey buzzed after the speeding car like a giant mosquito chasing its prey. When they got within a hundred yards, the flight engineer trained the chopper's onboard searchlight on the vehicle.

Dodge didn't need night-vision goggles now. He could see the shape of the vehicle clearly. Could see, as well, the startled face that turned up to stare at the hovering helicopter. While Digger divided his concentration between the instruments, the area ahead and the speeding vehicle, Dodge radioed flight ops.

"Rotor One, this is Rotor Eleven."

"Go ahead, Rotor Eleven."

"We've spotted a dark-colored sedan traveling south on 287, approximately six miles south of Bellvue. Please advise if there are any state or local law-enforcement personnel in the immediate area."

He was back with the answer in less than a minute.

"Negative, Rotor Eleven. The sheriff advises his closest cruiser is ten miles north of your present position. He's directing the cruiser to turn around."

"Roger, Rotor One. We'll stay with this…."

He broke off, his eyes narrowing as the passenger-side window lowered. A half second later a small burst of green flowered bright. Two more followed in quick succession.

"He's firing on us!" Instinctively, Digger jinked the stick and swung away. "The son of a bitch is firing on us!"

Dodge had his Beretta out of its holster in the next breath. "Bring her around, Digger."

"Jesus, Hamilton."

"Bring her around."

Swearing a blue streak, Digger tipped into a sharp bank and zoomed back toward the sedan.

"Steady…" Dodge ordered softly. "Steady…"

Whoever was at the window took aim again. The muzzle flashed bright green at the same instant Dodge fired. Although they presented a far larger target, previous generations of the Huey had taken heavier fire in every conflict since Vietnam. This one proved every bit as resilient.

A hole blossomed in the canopy just inches above Digger's head, but Dodge's shot inflicted considerably more damage. The Taurus's window shattered. The passenger was flung backward, across the seat. He must have slammed into the driver because the vehicle fishtailed wildly and spun around, once, twice. It was still spinning when Digger banked again and brought the Huey around.

Dodge was out of the cockpit before the skids touched. He raced for the vehicle just as the driver's door sprang open and a man leaped out. In the bright glare of the searchlight Dodge saw him crouch into a two-fisted shooter's stance.

"Barlow! Don't be a…"

He got off one shot before Dodge dropped him. He slammed against the car's hood and hung there for a second or two before sinking slowly to his knees.

Dodge reached him as he hit dirt and twisted the automatic from his grasp. The bastard wasn't dead, but then Dodge hadn't aimed to kill. A quick pat-down produced nothing more lethal than a cell phone. He tossed it aside and yanked open the Taurus's side door.

The passenger's body was sprawled grotesquely across the front console. There was no one in the backseat. Dodge reached down to pop the trunk lid. It lifted to reveal a dark, empty compartment.

Murder in his heart, he strode back to the man stretched out in the dirt. Barlow had crawled a few feet to retrieve his phone. His bloodied fingers fumbled at the keys.

Dodge's lips pulled back. "Calling your lawyer, you piece of crap? You're gonna need a good one."

Barlow stabbed the keys frantically. Disgusted, Dodge swung a boot and kicked the phone out of his hands. It sailed off into the darkness, the LCD panel a firefly of light, and Dodge went down on one knee.

"Where's Lara?"

Barlow gave his phone a last glance and angled his head around. Dodge could swear he saw a flicker of triumph in his eyes before they went cold.

"I don't know who the hell you're talking about, Major, but I do know this. You're the one who's going to need a good lawyer."

"Think so?"

"I know so." Grimacing, he pushed himself up on an elbow. "You swoop down out of the dark like that, send us off the road. We—my partner and I—had no idea who you were or what you wanted. We had to defend ourselves."

Dodge answered that by aiming the Beretta at his uninjured shoulder.

"Defend yourself against this. You got five seconds to tell me where Larissa Petrovna is. Then I pop your elbow. Five seconds after that, I go for a kneecap. If you're still not talking, I blow off your balls."

He meant it. Every word. Barlow must have realized that, because he threw a frantic look at the helicopter.

"Hey! Help me! This guy's nuts!"

"Four," Dodge counted. "Three. Two…"

Digger appeared at his side. "Yo, Hamilton!"

"Keep out of my line of fire," he warned. "This piece of slime is about to lose a few body parts."

"Don't make me no never mind if you bore a hole the size of South Dakota in him. But we just intercepted a flash on one of the police nets. An abandoned farmhouse a few miles off I-40 just went up in flames."

"*Where* off I-40?"

"Just south of the rest stop where we touched down earlier."

He hadn't taken his eyes off Barlow. The man didn't move so much as a muscle. He didn't have to. Dodge put it together in that instant.

The cell phone! He'd used it to signal another accomplice. Or trigger the fire.

Rage consumed him, so swift and fierce his finger tightened on the trigger. He came closer in that moment to going rogue than he would have believed possible. Digger pulled him back from the brink.

"I've radioed in our location. Police and medics are on the way. You leave Barlow with me and take the Huey."

* * *

Dodge swung into the pilot's seat and strapped in, thanking God for the ability to compartmentalize. Fear that Lara was trapped in the blazing farmhouse ate at his insides like acid, but he moved that fear to one side of his mind and flew with the other.

He could see the fire long before they reached it. Like a beacon of death, it lit up the night sky. He touched down in an open field some distance away and powered down the Huey before racing across the weed-filled field.

Half a dozen assorted emergency vehicles had drawn into a half circle, their powerful spots aimed at the farmhouse. The roof had collapsed in on itself. Flames consumed the two remaining walls. Smoke rolled thick and black into the night sky.

Dodge made straight for the helmeted firefighter standing beside the pumper, radio in hand as he directed operations.

"Major Petrovna?"

"What?"

"The missing Russian woman? Have you found her?"

The firefighter looked him up and down, taking in his uniform and the name tag on his chest, before he answered.

"We found her."

Dodge brought his shoulders back and braced for the worst.

"Or more correctly, she found us."

He jerked his chin toward a highway patrol car parked at the perimeter of the scene. Dodge's heart tripped when he spotted a smoke-blackened figure huddled in a blanket in the backseat.

He didn't stop to analyze the emotion that grabbed him by the throat and squeezed hard. Later he would realize it was a combination of relief and thanksgiving and a feeling that belonged between the lines of a poem. All he thought of at that moment, however, was getting his arms around her and never letting go.

She hadn't seen him arrive but did see him break through the ring of vehicles and charge in her direction. Flinging off the blanket, she scrambled out of the squad car and threw herself at him. Then the rigid, always-in-control ice maiden scared the hell out of him by bursting into loud, noisy sobs.

"Lara. Sweetheart." He crushed her against his chest, rocking her, soothing her, feeling as helpless as men always did around a sobbing woman. "It's okay. You're okay."

He'd murmured the inanity before its reality hit him. Swearing, he grasped her upper arms.

"You are okay, aren't you?"

He made a frantic search, didn't spot any bandages. Nothing except soot and grime and a flood of tears.

"Lara, speak to me. Tell me if he hurt you."

That got through to her. Those lake-blue eyes flashed fury beneath their watery sheen. She spit out a stream of Russian, caught herself and switched to English.

"The pig. The filthy pig. He turns his Taser on me and ties me to a chair and leaves me to burn like my Yuri and Elena Dimitri. We must find him, Dodge, and when we do, I will rip out his throat."

"We've got him."

His fierce comment didn't register. Probably because she'd gone from fury to stark terror in the space of a single heartbeat.

"Katya!" She grabbed the front of his flight suit, dug her fingers in. "Barlow sends me a picture of Katya."

"I saw it."

"He has friends in Moscow, Dodge. FSB friends. They will hurt her. I asked my colonel to take her and keep her safe, but they will find her and hurt her if I speak of what he did."

"No, they won't."

"They will!" Her fingers dug deeper. "They have

ways. Many ways. I must go home at once. I must protect my daughter."

"Lara, listen to me. He won't hurt your daughter. He has no reason to."

"He has every reason!" She tore out of his hold, incredulous at his seeming incomprehension. "He started the fire that took my husband. Last night he tries to kill me."

"And until we have Katya safe, we'll make damn sure he thinks he succeeded."

"What do you say?"

He speared a glance at the still-blazing farmhouse. No media on the scene yet, only police and fire personnel. He'd make sure that when the media did descend, every agency involved in this operation sang from the same sheet of music.

With a grim smile, he turned back to Lara. "You're dead, sweetheart. Better get used to it, because you're going to stay that way for a while."

Chapter 12

"You're gonna wear a hole in that floor. I don't mind, you understand. Just don't want you to trip over ragged floorboards."

Sam Hamilton's laconic comment spun Lara around. She glared at him before turning her ire on the honey-haired woman sitting at the kitchen table with him.

"I have been hiding here at the Double H for four days. Four nights! The world thinks my charred bones were found in the farmhouse. My mission was terminated. The others on my team have gone home. Barlow has been allowed to leave the hospital. Yet all you can tell me is that Dodge is working with

Colonel Zacharov to uncover the pigs in FSB who take money from Barlow."

"You know what we know," the woman responded.

The calm reply took some of the heat from Lara's simmering impatience. This one was used to being active, too. She'd graduated from the U.S. academy for air-force officers. Then she'd flown jets. Big ones. Now she worked for the same shadowy agency Dodge did. Even her code name sparked interest. Rebel. She'd shared enough of her past during the days they'd been at the Double H for Lara to believe the name was well and truly earned.

Yet you would not think her an undercover agent to look at her, Lara thought with a nasty little dart of envy. More like a sultry model, in those black leather pants and leather jacket with so many silver studs. She wore both with the sinuous grace of a panther. Small wonder the face of Dodge's cousin, Sam, had lit up like a child with a new toy when she arrived.

Even less wonder that Lara felt like a colorless wraith in comparison. She'd scrubbed the soot from her pores and dressed in jeans and a red flannel shirt Sam had appropriated from the clothes Dodge kept at the ranch for his visits. Her hair had been washed and brushed to a silvery sheen. She'd even applied some lip gloss that Rebel had given her to use. Despite the touches of color, she couldn't compete with the other woman's blatant sensuality.

She had come to keep Lara company. That was the bland explanation Dodge had given before he thrust his hands through Lara's hair for a kiss that left her reeling, then promptly disappeared.

To keep her in her coffin was closer to the truth, Lara fumed. As far as the rest of the world was concerned, she'd perished in the fire. She could only pray that no one had told Katya her mother was dead. Dodge had promised they would not. Colonel Zacharov, too, when he'd called to assure Lara that he had her daughter tucked away in his *dacha* outside Moscow.

And there she would stay until Dodge and Zacharov and top officials from both governments rooted out the rot on both sides of the Atlantic. For that, they needed Lara to remain dead and Barlow to believe he'd silenced the only witness who could pin him to a deadly fire.

They were monitoring the bastard's calls. Watching his every move. Tracking down every suspicious contact. While she sat here doing nothing!

Frustrated all over again, Lara resumed her pacing. Long, stalking steps took her from the stove to the sink with its breath-stealing view of the corrals and snow-peaked mountains beyond. So she was the first one to spot the vehicle that turned onto the long, winding road that led to the ranch house. A moment later it bumped over the cattle guard and set off a low, beeping alarm inside the house.

Rebel extracted a weapon from her boot and flowed out of her chair in one fluid move. Sam snatched up the rifle propped beside the table. It was one of two he'd kept loaded and ready over the past few days.

"Lara, you need to stay put," he said quietly. "Let us check this out."

Enough was enough. She'd not been trained to stay put. Jaw set, she stalked over to the spare rifle.

"Jesus, Lara! Dodge will skin me alive if I let you get caught in a shoot-out."

She slapped his hand away. "And I will skin you alive if you do not."

"You, er, know how to use that?"

Her chin came up. The proud blood of her ancestors rang in her reply. "I am descended from Cossacks."

Sam sent Rebel a silent plea.

"Don't look at me, big guy. I'm not going to tangle with a Cossack."

Feeling more kinship with the other woman than she had since her arrival, Lara took up a position at one window. Rebel covered the other. Sam kept one eye on the door and another on the monitor showing four different surveillance screens. When the hidden camera panned the driver's side window of the vehicle, he let out a satisfied grunt.

"It's Dodge."

"And Blade," Rebel added, eyeing the screen.

Lara's pent-up emotions shot to a fever pitch. She had yet to come to grips with the chaotic feelings Dodge roused in her. He annoyed her intensely at times. Reminded her all too sharply of their different loyalties at others. Then he swept her into his arms and she found herself almost—almost!—believing those differences could be overcome.

That mix of confusion, hope and eager anticipation washed over her again and propelled her out the door. She waited with Sam and Rebel until the dusty vehicle spun to a halt. Dodge climbed out and tipped two fingers to his hat brim, then turned away.

Lara's joyous anticipation took a dip. She'd imagined this moment so many times in the past three days. She had *not* imagined that he would nod and turn his back on her. She stood stiffly, refusing to let her hurt show, until the rear passenger door slammed and Dodge reappeared—holding the hand of a small, wide-eyed girl clutching a stuffed pony almost as big as she was.

Lara's legs went weak. Tears rushed to her throat.

All she could do was sink to her knees and open her arms.

"Mama!" Shrieking, Katya flew across the gravel drive. "Mama!"

Dodge had figured nothing could give him more satisfaction than personally delivering the news that he and Colonel Zacharov had squeezed confessions from three highly placed FSB officers that they'd taken hefty bribes from Hank Barlow.

He'd figured wrong, however. The incandescent joy on Lara's face as she smothered her child with kisses relegated Barlow to no more than an annoying blip on the radar screen.

Rebel sauntered over to join her fellow operatives. "You done good," she murmured to Dodge. "And you…"

Arching a brow, she studied the bruise darkening the left side of Blade's chin.

"Forget to duck?"

"Something like that."

"Well, don't expect me to kiss your boo-boo and make it better."

She turned away and missed the sudden gleam in Blade's eyes. Dodge caught it, however, and hoped he was nowhere in the vicinity when the whatever the hell these two had bubbling below the surface exploded.

Then he swung his attention back to Lara and felt everything inside him turn to Silly Putty.

It wasn't until hours later that mother and daughter could be separated. While Blade entertained Katya with a trip to the barn to see the horses, the others clustered around the kitchen table with the remains of supper still in the sink and a second pot of coffee brewing. If either Rebel or Sam noticed that Lara's hand had found a home in Dodge's, they didn't comment on it.

"I'll say this for your Colonel Zacharov. The man's a bulldog," Dodge related with a wry grin. "He'd already ferreted out the prime suspects when Blade and I got there. All it took was some, uh, intense interrogation to give Zacharov enough for an extradition request on Barlow."

"What is this extradition?"

"They want us to send him back to Moscow to stand trial for black marketeering, bribing public officials, and for the murder of Elena Dimitri, your husband and the others who died in the fire."

"And the United States will do this?"

"After we nail him for attempted murder and arson here in the States."

"How long will it take for such matters to happen?"

"We'll try to speed the process along, but Barlow's going to hire a battery of lawyers. It could take months."

"And until then, Katya must be protected."

Dodge rubbed the side of his nose. "Yeah, well, the colonel and I talked about that. He thinks, and I agree, that both you and Katya should continue to lay low until Barlow's in a cage."

"I cannot remain dead for a month! I have a job, responsibilities, people under my supervision."

"We talked about that, too. Just how long has it been since you took any vacation time?"

"Katya and I went to the Black Sea just last year."

"For three days, according to your boss."

"We went to the Urals to ski the year before."

"Over a long weekend."

"How do you know this?" she demanded, exasperated.

"Like I said, your colonel and I had a chat. We think you should…"

"Yes, yes. You told me what you think." Her chin came up, and a hint of her former ice coated her reply. "I do not need men making decisions for me."

Rebel grinned. "You tell 'em, girl."

Ignoring the aside, Dodge leaned forward and

held Lara's hand captive. "Zacharov cares about you, Larissa Petrovna. I care about you."

He didn't need Rebel's disgusted snort to know that had come out with about as much kick as week-old chili. Or the cool look Lara gave him as she pushed away from the table.

"I must see to Katya."

Sam eyed her retreating back and shook his head. "Smooth, Hoss. Real smooth."

"Hope you do better next time," Rebel drawled.

"I will," Dodge vowed.

He waited to make his move until Lara had tucked Katya in bed. The oversize stuffed horse Dodge had picked up at the Cheyenne airport snuggled beside her. Her tentative smile when he came to say good-night pulled at something deep inside him.

He returned the smile and leaned a shoulder against the doorjamb while Lara crooned softly to her daughter in Russian, smoothing her hair, stroking her cheek, as if she couldn't get enough of touching her. After the long plane ride and excitement of seeing her mother again, Katya dropped right off.

Still Lara sat with her. She knew Dodge stood behind her, knew she owed him much for helping to put the ghosts of the past to rest. Yet now that her initial euphoria had passed, she felt almost reluctant to face him. It would be hard to say goodbye. Harder still if she and Katya stayed here for weeks, seeing him whenever he could spare time from his duties. Best to break it off now, while she could go home with only an ache inside her for what might have been.

Drawing in a long breath, she smoothed her daughter's hair a last time, rose and faced him. Soundlessly, he held out the flannel-lined jacket she'd appropriated as her own.

"Moon's full," he said quietly. "Let's talk outside."

The sky was an endless sea of stars. They were so brilliant, these Wyoming stars. And the moon hanging low in the dark velvet sky was round and full and bright. Lara breathed in the sharp, clean tang of pine resin and walked with Dodge to the now empty corral.

Pushing her hands in the jacket pockets for warmth, she leaned against the corral's top bar and studied his face, shadowed by his hat brim. So strong, so confident, so ruggedly handsome. To forestall argument, she smiled and shook her head.

"Dodge, I thank you from the bottom of my heart for all you have done. You and Sam and the others. But you know I cannot stay here."

"Not forever," he agreed. "But certainly long

enough for us to figure out where we go from here."

"Where *can* we go? You're a spy. You work for an agency even the FSB has no data on. I'm an officer in the Russian Air Force. I will have to answer many questions about you—about *us*—when I go home."

"All you have to do is tell them the truth."

"Tell them I was so reckless? So lost to all sense of duty that I…that I…"

"Consorted with the enemy?"

Her brow furrowed. "What is this, 'consorted'?"

"Stopped his heart with your smile." He braced his hands on the top bar, caging her between them. "Kissed him until he couldn't remember his name. Made love with him a dozen times."

"A dozen? We slept together but once!"

"True, but the night's young." He brushed his mouth over hers. "And I intend to make the most of it."

Her palms flattened on his chest. He could see the want in her face, and the regret.

"We must be rational, Dodge. We come from different worlds."

"It's the world we make for each other, and for Katya, that counts from here on out."

"It's impossible!"

His mouth made another lazy pass over hers. "How do you know unless we give it a shot?"

She ached to wrap her arms around his neck. To bring that so-skilled mouth crushing down on hers. To feel his hard, muscled body against and on and in hers just once more. Instead, she bunched her fists and kept them stiff at her side.

"I cannot live with you passing through my life— and Katya's—whenever business or chance or whim brings you to Moscow. I want more for her, Dodge. For myself."

"I wasn't planning on just passing through. I'm asking you to marry me, Larissa Petrovna."

"What!"

He had to grin at her openmouthed shock.

"Colonel Zacharov and I worked it out. He thinks you're perfect to fill the assistant defense attaché slot at the Russian Embassy in D.C. That'll keep you on this side of the Atlantic for the next four years. After that, I have business interests in Moscow that could keep me there for four or five. Then we'll see what comes."

Her head spun with disbelief, with confusion, with the first electric sparks of excitement. "The assistant attaché position is that of a lieutenant colonel," she protested.

"Zacharov seems to think you deserve a promotion

for nailing a mass murderer and busting up a black-market ring involving several FSB officers. He also thinks it would be good for you and Katya to remain in the States for a while, until Barlow and his buddies are behind bars."

"But…"

"Katya thinks it's a good idea, too. Especially after I promised to get her some Silly Bandz and bring her to the Double H for every vacation."

"But…"

"What the hell *are* Silly Bandz, anyway? A rock group?"

"No, no! My God, Hamilton, you do not give me time to catch my breath."

"That's the general idea."

He smiled down at her, and the denials piling up by the dozens in her thoughts didn't make it to her lips.

"I love you, Larissa Petrovna."

He framed her face with his palms. His touch was warm against her cheeks, and strong, and so achingly tender.

"I love your dedication to your duty," he said softly. "Your coolness under pressure. Your incredible bravery and the savage way you fight to protect you and yours. I love the heart that beats inside the body I've lusted for since the moment we met."

She stared up at him, her eyes a dark cobalt-blue in the moonlight. They showed doubt, amazement, confusion still. But the ghosts were gone, Dodge saw with fierce satisfaction. If he'd done nothing else, he'd helped her put them to rest.

"I loved once," she said after a long moment. "With all my heart. I never thought to find such a gift again."

Her smile came then. Wide and full.

"It will not be easy, having me as wife. These differences you brush aside so lightly go bone-deep in both of us. But I tell you this, Dodge Hamilton, I ache for you in ways I never ached before."

With a silent vow to keep her aching for the next fifty or sixty years, Dodge folded her into his arms and sealed their personal treaty.

Epilogue

The wedding was an elegant affair. The entire Russian embassy staff filled the pews on the bride's side of the flower-draped aisles. Squeezed in among the dignitaries in the front row was the woman who'd taken care of Katya during Lara's military absences. Colonel Zacharov had arranged a visa and had flown her to Washington several weeks ago to assist the embassy's assistant defense attaché as she adjusted to her new position. Zacharov was at the church, too, resplendent in his dress uniform with medals adorning one entire side of his chest.

Dodge's family, friends, military associates and fellow operatives filled the pews on the other side of the aisle. His family and friends had come to share his joy. Sam led the pack, riding herd on an assortment of sisters, aunts, cousins and their numerous offspring.

The OMEGA cadre, on the other hand, had come primarily to see the Russian officer who'd roped, hog-tied and was about to put a ring through Hamilton's nose. A fat wad of bills had changed hands among the operatives at the previous night's bachelor party. When the losers of the pool had forked over several hundred to a grinning Victoria Talbot, she'd scooped up the cash and freely admitted she'd gained the inside track during the time she'd spent cloistered with Major Petrovna at the Double H. After watching Dodge and Lara together, she'd known it was only a matter of weeks before the Russian brought ole love-'em-and-leave-'em Hamilton to his knees.

The bond that had sprung up between Dodge and Lara's daughter had certainly moved things along, as well. Katya wouldn't be parted from the giant stuffed pony Dodge had bought her—until he and Sam had trotted out a real live pony. The little girl had squealed with joy and scrambled into the saddle unaided. From that moment, she'd held an unshakable lock on the hearts of both Dodge and *Dyadya* Sam.

She was right there at the altar with Dodge and her mama. She clung to his hand and that of her mother while the two adults exchanged vows. Her gap-toothed grin when they marched down the aisle in the recessional displayed beaming joy.

The reception that followed the wedding was much less formal. Nick and Mackenzie Jensen had offered their home for the affair. The colonial-era tobacco-plantation mansion was only a few miles outside D.C. The gorgeously restored and enlarged house provided easy circulation for the large crowd. The tree-shaded yard gave the kids plenty of room to romp in.

Nick and Mackenzie's twin boys squealed with delight when their "cousin"—Maggie and Adam's adopted grandson—got them soaring on rope swings. Katya hung back, clinging to her uncle Sam's hand until a delicate, doe-eyed girl her own age approached.

"I am Mei Lin," the girl announced. "Number-one daughter of Jill-An and Cal-Han."

At Katya's blank look, Mei Lin gestured to the couple standing with Dodge and Lara. The woman's belly swelled against the front of her dress. The man with his arm looped loosely around her waist looked down at her with the same silly expression that came over Dodge when he regarded Katya's mama.

Deeming it safe to release her death grip on Sam's hand, she followed the little girl to a child-size table set under the branches of a majestic elm. Within moments, they were pouring "tea" and chattering away in a mix of English, Russian and Chinese.

Gillian Ridgeway Callahan smiled as her gaze rested on the two girls. The oldest offspring of Maggie and Adam Ridgway, she fingered a gold Chinese character embedded in a bezel of rare blue jade. She had her father's glossy black hair and, Lara had discovered, had once been a part of the same clandestine organization as Dodge and so many others present.

"I told you the girls would hit it off," she said to Lara with a smile. "You and Dodge should buy somewhere close to us so Mei Lin and Katya can play together."

Lara nodded but couldn't commit to permanent living arrangements.

"Everything has happened so fast," she said with a rueful glance at her husband. "First Dodge tells me that Katya and I must stay at his ranch for several months while Hank Barlow is brought to justice. Then, in almost the next breath, he says it's done and we are to be married."

"That's because my bulldog brother muscled his way onto the case," Gillian replied, laughing. "We called him Tank as a kid because he always charged straight ahead, bowling over any and all obstacles in his path. He does the same now as an assistant U.S. district attorney."

"I hear he's thinking about following in his father, mother and sister's footsteps," her husband commented.

"Oh, Lord!" Gillian's jaw sagged. "OMEGA will never be the same."

Four pairs of eyes locked on the tall, broad-shouldered attorney engaging Victoria Talbot in a bantering conversation. Rebel's honey-blond hair spilled over her shoulders as she laughed up at him. Blade stood on Rebel's other side. Judging by his expression, he didn't appear to get the joke.

"This could prove interesting," Dodge murmured. "Real interesting," he added as Lightning approached the trio.

He'd been with OMEGA long enough to read the signs. Lightning's smile was easy and his manner casual, but a tip of his chin soon sent Rebel and Blade toward the house. A few moments later, Lara noticed Colonel Zacharov heading inside, as well.

She turned to Dodge, a question in her eyes. "Do we join them?"

His first instinct was to nod. His second, to trust Lightning. Grinning, he framed his bride's face with his callused palms.

"If whatever they're talking about concerns us,

we'll hear about it soon enough. And if it doesn't, we have a honeymoon to enjoy. How soon do you think we can say our goodbyes?"

"Dodge! We only just arrived."

"So?"

"Go," Gillian instructed, laughing. "If OMEGA wants you, they know how to get a hold of you."

Dodge took her at her word and swept his protesting wife into his arms.

"Y'all excuse us," he announced to the company at large. "The major—correction, the *colonel* and Katya and I have a suite waiting us at Walt Disney's Animal Kingdom Lodge."

The guests hooted and applauded as an unabashed Dodge swooped out with the two females who had become the nexus of his world.

* * * * *

Author's Note

I first started researching this book almost a decade ago but put it aside to work on other projects. Since then, however, I've followed with interest the efforts by several successive U.S. administrations to negotiate a new treaty to reduce the world's nuclear arsenal.

Talk about timing! I had dusted off this book and started reworking it just about the time the president signed a new START treaty and sent it to the Senate for ratification. Congress voted to ratify the treaty just as I typed THE END. Kinda makes me feel as if I were a part of history!

And speaking of history, don't miss the next Code Name: Danger adventure. *Double Deception,*

available August 2011, takes Rebel and Blade deep
into the dark underbelly of the black-market art world
in search of priceless amber panels looted by the
Nazis during WWII.

All my best,

Harlequin®

ROMANTIC
SUSPENSE

COMING NEXT MONTH

Available June 28, 2011

#1663 JUST A COWBOY
Conard County: The Next Generation
Rachel Lee

#1664 PRIVATE JUSTICE
The Kelley Legacy
Marie Ferrarella

#1665 SOLDIER'S LAST STAND
H.O.T. Watch
Cindy Dees

#1666 SWORN TO PROTECT
Native Country
Kimberly Van Meter

You can find more information on upcoming
Harlequin® titles, free excerpts and more at
www.HarlequinInsideRomance.com.

REQUEST YOUR FREE BOOKS!
2 FREE NOVELS PLUS 2 FREE GIFTS!

ROMANTIC
SUSPENSE

Sparked by Danger, Fueled by Passion.

YES! Please send me 2 FREE Harlequin® Romantic Suspense novels and my 2 FREE gifts (gifts are worth about $10). After receiving them, if I don't wish to receive any more books, I can return the shipping statement marked "cancel." If I don't cancel, I will receive 4 brand-new novels every month and be billed just $4.24 per book in the U.S. or $4.99 per book in Canada. That's a saving of at least 15% off the cover price! It's quite a bargain! Shipping and handling is just 50¢ per book in the U.S. and 75¢ per book in Canada.* I understand that accepting the 2 free books and gifts places me under no obligation to buy anything. I can always return a shipment and cancel at any time. Even if I never buy another book, the two free books and gifts are mine to keep forever.

240/340 SDN FC95

Name	(PLEASE PRINT)	
Address		Apt. #
City	State/Prov.	Zip/Postal Code

Signature (if under 18, a parent or guardian must sign)

Mail to the Reader Service:
IN U.S.A.: P.O. Box 1867, Buffalo, NY 14240-1867
IN CANADA: P.O. Box 609, Fort Erie, Ontario L2A 5X3

Not valid for current subscribers to Harlequin Romantic Suspense books.

Want to try two free books from another line?
Call 1-800-873-8635 or visit www.ReaderService.com.

* Terms and prices subject to change without notice. Prices do not include applicable taxes. Sales tax applicable in N.Y. Canadian residents will be charged applicable taxes. Offer not valid in Quebec. This offer is limited to one order per household. All orders subject to credit approval. Credit or debit balances in a customer's account(s) may be offset by any other outstanding balance owed by or to the customer. Please allow 4 to 6 weeks for delivery. Offer available while quantities last.

Your Privacy—The Reader Service is committed to protecting your privacy. Our Privacy Policy is available online at www.ReaderService.com or upon request from the Reader Service.

We make a portion of our mailing list available to reputable third parties that offer products we believe may interest you. If you prefer that we not exchange your name with third parties, or if you wish to clarify or modify your communication preferences, please visit us at www.ReaderService.com/consumerschoice or write to us at Reader Service Preference Service, P.O. Box 9062, Buffalo, NY 14269. Include your complete name and address.

HRS11

USA TODAY *bestselling author B.J. Daniels*
takes you on a trip to Whitehorse, Montana,
and the Chisholm Cattle Company.

RUSTLED

Available July 2011 from Harlequin Intrigue.

As the dust settled, Dawson got his first good look at the rustler. A pair of big Montana sky-blue eyes glared up at him from a face framed by blond curls.

A woman rustler?

"You have to let me go," she hollered as the roar of the stampeding cattle died off in the distance.

"So you can finish stealing my cattle? I don't think so." Dawson jerked the woman to her feet.

She reached for the gun strapped to her hip hidden under her long barn jacket.

He grabbed the weapon before she could, his eyes narrowing as he assessed her. "How many others are there?" he demanded, grabbing a fistful of her jacket. "I think you'd better start talking before I tear into you."

She tried to fight him off, but he was on to her tricks and pinned her to the ground. He was suddenly aware of the soft curves beneath the jean jacket she wore under her coat.

"You have to listen to me." She ground out the words from between her gritted teeth. "You have to let me go. If you don't they will come back for me and they will kill you. There are too many of them for you to fight off alone. You won't stand a chance and I don't want your blood on my hands."

"I'm touched by your concern for me. Especially after you just tried to pull a gun on me."

"I wasn't going to shoot you."

Dawson hauled her to her feet and walked her the rest of the way to his horse. Reaching into his saddlebag, he pulled out a length of rope.

"You can't tie me up."

He pulled her hands behind her back and began to tie her wrists together.

"If you let me go, I can keep them from coming back," she said. "You have my word." She let out an unladylike curse. "I'm just trying to save your sorry neck."

"And I'm just going after my cattle."

"Don't you mean your boss's cattle?"

"Those cattle are mine."

"*You're* a Chisholm?"

"Dawson Chisholm. And you are…?"

"Everyone calls me Jinx."

He chuckled. "I can see why."

*Bronco busting, falling in love…it's all in a day's work.
Look for the rest of their story in*

RUSTLED

*Available July 2011 from Harlequin Intrigue
wherever books are sold.*

HIEXP0711R